Kittens in the Boiler

Delphine LeCompte

Merry Xmas
Andrew! 2005
Love Laurel
xoxoxoxo

THIEVES JARGON PRESS *** SALEM, MA

This is a work of fiction. Names, characters, places, and incidents either are the product of the author's imagination or are used fictitiously. Any resemblance to actual events, locales, organizations, or persons, living or dead, is entirely coincidental and beyond the intent of either the author or the publisher.

Some parts of this novel have previously appeared in different form in the following journals: *Thieves Jargon, Laura Hird, Unlikely Stories, Muse Apprentice Guild, Passenger May, Cyanide, Bullet* and *Mad Swirl*.

ISBN: 0-9770750-0-1

Thieves Jargon Press
PO Box 2064
Salem, MA 01970

Printed in the United States of America

First edition, first printing: September, 2005

Dedication

to my faithful,reliable and
determined editor

to my sweet,doe-eyed and
saintlike scottish brother

to my moody,sultry and
tanned soulmate

to my voracious,crossbow-
wielding neighbour

to my forgiving,fickle and
endearing sheffielder friend

to my patient,moustached and
dreamy flemish arts teacher
who has made a difference

to the manic street preachers

for nick cave

THE BATTLE AGAINST FOX EVIL / blame my gene pool, blame my parents, blame my catholic teachers, blame the sleazy nurses, blame the inadequate doctors, blame the horny shrinks, blame the kinky clerics, blame the sugar, blame the glue, blame the booze, blame the bedsit, blame the television, blame freud, blame labour, blame the 21st century, blame the supermarket, blame the friends turned yuppies, blame the twisted poofs, blame the north sea, blame the climate, blame the bible, blame the rash on my left arm, blame my wicked stepsister, blame the moon, blame the gloomy donkeys, blame the smiths, blame the insipid novels, blame the westerns, blame the flatulent family dog, blame my short tempered grandfather, blame my red scarf, blame my working class background, blame my fickle lovers, blame britpop, blame kurt cobain, bang bang bang, but don't blame me, blame blame blame someone else.

one

WEE WOLVES AND BIG PERVS / i was brought up by wolves, the cunt that spawned me was seventeen and addicted to crack and she couldn't take care of me so she left me in a forest where she hoped i'd soon be eaten by boars or wolves, but i wasn't, the wolves found me and fed me and then taught me how to take care of myself, they taught me many things; i was ten years old when them rotten twisted adults accidentally found me, they didn't teach me much, they didn't talk to me at all cos they didn't think i would understand; they tied and gagged and beat and raped me cos they didn't think i'd tell on them; i ran away many times, back to the forest, back to my lupine family, but they wouldn't have me anymore cos i smelled like a rotten twisted human being, and i wouldn't have survived anyway cos my teeth had grown dull and i was gradually losing the hair on my back and belly and i no longer devoured rabbits and wee boys, i'd become a miserable minging orphan girl, and that's what i still am today; in my daydreams i am very lupine, and so is everyone else, we don't bark, we howl, and we roam the streets at night and devour dodgy creatures; of course this was all a long time ago, the forest and the wolves i mean, and i write stories now and i stack milk bottles and suck cock for a living, which are all very human things to do, but i still miss those hairy bellies and all that mammal warmth; i bought a fluffy stuffed rabbit yesterday and tried to devour it, but i nearly choked on it, and if i still had something left of a real wolf in me i wouldn't have bought that rabbit, i would have just devoured it there and then, and the shop assistants would have backed away in horror instead of asking me if the rabbit needed to be wrapped; nobody in this dreary coastal town speaks my language, and i don't speak theirs, they think i'm a bit thick but that's my charm, and they think i'm innocent and that's another one of my charms; but i'm not innocent, i just don't say much, i don't see the point in making conversation with people who are about to rape me, and all the people i meet are about to massacre my genitals; that's why i'm hiding in this place where the dunes merge into the forest, there are no pervs here, all the pervs are watching the fireworks; there's someone staggering towards me, it's wee andy and he's bleeding, it's only his nose, why's he staggering then?? he's such a drama queen, i'm just gonna ignore him, but i can't ignore wee fucking andy, i fancy wee fucking andy; he's telling how some ned punched him in the face, just like that, cos he didn't like the way wee andy's dressed, and i can see his point, why does the poof always have to wear so many beads and brooches and bracelets and tight poof jeans and whatnot, can't he dress like a man?? his father killed himself when he was four and he was brought up by women, but that's still no excuse to wear so much junk jewelry; i stroke his hair, we are listening to oasis and drinking vodka, the sea is rumbling somewhere in the pitch dark, why were there fireworks anyway? i ask wee andy; he doesn't know, maybe there's no reason? maybe they just wanted to give all those suicidal coastal people a treat? they're gonna become spoiled if the government gives them too many fireworks, it'll all backfire, if they're really suicidal these fireworks will only incite them, soon there'll be no people left in the coastal town, nobody but us, wouldn't that be bliss? would you fuck me if i was the only person left in this town? do you miss your father? do you sometimes wish you were brought up by wolves like i was? do you think you'd be a different person? do you reckon we'd be friends? the sky is pink, i'm glad i'm sober enough to see it, cos it's a spectacular coastal sunrise, when i stand on one of the pillboxes i can see a dirty rusty ship that's heading for france, wee andy's sleeping on a slaughtered tree, its branches are all raised to the sky like it's pleading with some cunt above to resurrect it rather than let poofs and winos crash on it; i gather my stuff and steal away out of the dunes and into the forest, it's a wee forest and it's infested with obnoxious white kids and overweight labradors.

ROSES AND MONDAYS / i'm not really an orphan, i just tell people that i am cos it sounds so much more romantic than having to tell them that my mother ran off with a french philosopher and that my father is a spiteful busker who treats me like i'm some obsessive stalker, but i'm not, i'm his daughter and i think his songs are pish; then i was dropped into this decadent environment in which my grandparents thrived: snuff movies, pornography, orgies; i was always hidden under the table watching those despicable adults with their saggy flesh

and vulgar patter hurting each other, intentionally, corrupting each other, smothering
anything remotely resembling innocence, breeding rapists, taking pride in sucking rich cock; i cried a lot under that table, the family dog was always with me and i told him, like i'm telling my sheffielder angel right now: "i'm never gonna take pride in sucking rich cock and you're the only creature i trust".

MY LITTLE VIOLENT EMPIRE / i've been indoors for a week now, but i'm not hiding, one can't hide in a building with no front door, a building occupied by five junkies, a nymphomaniac, two psycho dykes and a stuttering traumatised armenian, they all want something from me, and they all have their little sycophantic manipulative ways to set one up against the other, all i ever wanted was a quiet place, smiths songs and some random sex from time to time, and i got this: prostitution, a drinking problem, sleazy cops, scabby cocks, a russian cow killer and a noel gallagher obsession, i'm liking it, the world outside is so much safer than this brutal hive, but this is the only hive that's got something real to offer: i get shagged here, i get drugged, i get drunk, i get paid, i get beaten up, i get stabbed, i get threatened, i get praised, i get asked for advice, i get mugged, i get bored, i get frightened, everything's right here and i cannot get lost, every bleeding night this hysterical nymphet throws herself in front of my door where she writhes and twists and coils and slams her fists against my door howling and moaning about made-up rapes, imaginary abusive fathers, friends she never had that were brutally murdered by hirsute psycho-dealers, her parents put her away in a mental ward, if i had a daughter like that i'd bludgeon her with a sledgehammer and it'd save us all lots of money and time, maybe i'd get a peaceful night, just maybe, but ach, she always manages to strike a chord or maybe i'm just bored or maybe i'm just gloating, but i have to open my door, take her in my arms and stroke her hair gently; every bleeding night a traumatised armenian runs up and down the stairs bawling against horrendous specters and all the while he is cutting his chest with a broken beer bottle and rubbing himself against the walls, walls that have become quite an impressive guestbook: blood from vicious junkie brawls and from the nymphet who smears it from inside her legs, spunk, dried-up vomit and spit, flecks of shit, manics quotes in black marker (my contribution), fibres and fingerprints, so many nationalities, so many languages, all equally fucked-up and all staying in.

THE WEE MIDDLE CLASS CUNT AND THE FUCKED-UP ORPHAN GIRL / i met wee andy for the first time at the orphanage, of course the smug middle class cunt was only accompanying his smug middle class mother who happened to be my social worker, the cunt who failed to get me a foster family; i took an instant disliking to wee andy, he stared at us as if we were zoo animals, which we were to him, an exotic species, alluring but frightening, i was the most dangerous animal of the pack, he accompanied his mother every wednesday from then on, maybe it was some kind of wry middle class lesson his bloody mother the fucking inefficient social worker wanted to teach him, "there are kids out there who are worse off than you, so be fucking grateful for being part of such a supportive warm loving family", or maybe it was more in the lines of "there are malicious fucked-up kids out there, you can't befriend them but you have to learn how to deal with them", yeah that'll be more like it; he did befriend me though, he seemed to be quite fond of me, right from the first time we met, i never understood why; i spat in his face that first time, the wee curious cunt had asked me if i hated my parents, sentimental middle class bollocks like that, as if there was time to think in such terms, pffff, wee deluded cunt, and i spat in his face but he never finked on me, not that it redeemed the smug middle class cunt, cos he was probably just terrified to be beaten up by me; i looked forward to those wednesday afternoons, i would read music mags and he would sit opposite me and rant about obscure indie bands, trying to impress and placate me, and i would ignore him until i looked up at him one day and said: "middle class cunts shouldn't listen to indie music", which was bollocks of course cos most indie music is made by middle class cunts anyway, but i didn't want some wee smug over-privileged middle class twat to claim my music, "what are middle class cunts supposed to listen to then?", "jazz, i suppose", the wee cunt somehow found that hilarious, i remember his idiotic laughter reverberating against the bare walls of the canteen, it was probably the most cheerful laughter i'd ever heard in that canteen, quite possibly the only laughter, and i loathed myself for softening, and i loathed the wee cunt who caused all these bloody useless tender feelings inside me, "middle class cunts aren't supposed to listen to any music at all, they're supposed to get degrees in psychology and fuck up the lives of orphan girls even more, lives they only know out of text books and sentimental middle class films that get it all wrong", "but i'm only thirteen"," that's no fucking excuse", and i hit the wee sanctimonious bastard to the ground and that was our first conversation finished, the next wednesday he'd brought a mix tape with him, he'd tastelessly called it "orphan mix tape", "why don't you fucking bring me a foster mix tape next time, wee insensitive middle class cunt?!" it was a nice enough mix tape nonetheless, i heard the manics for the first time and i badly obsessed over nicky wire which suited everyone at the home fine cos it meant that i did all the hoovering for two years, i even bought a rock'n'roll star vacuum cleaner and i spray-painted manics quotes on it, and eventually i slept with it until one spiteful orphan girl trashed it; every wednesday wee andy brought me presents, making me feel like i was some kind of charity case, he probably meant well in his sad little unimaginative middle class way, but it was humiliating, and all the other orphan kids were laughing at me, and the presents were pointless anyway cos i had to share them; i never shared my mix tape with them malicious fucked-up orphan kids though, i kept it with me all the time, i listened to it all the time, it wasn't comforting or soothing, thankfully, cos i wasn't looking for comfort, it was fucking anger and mayhem and despair and sorrow, all of which i wallowed in, i felt awful but defiant, i cut myself compulsively, and when i told the wee thick cunt how the tape affected me he was horrified, when really i was only thanking him and he only should have said "my pleasure", but try explaining that to an overprivileged unimaginative middle class twat, it's no use; after a few months wee andy started to come more often, without his mother, i bet the sanctimonious bitch didn't even know of these little visits, i often wondered if this was just wee andy's pathetic middle class way of rebelling against his mother, befriending a fucked up orphan girl, but it didn't really matter, he annoyed the fuck out of me but i enjoyed his company, i loved being a total cunt to him, throwing abuse at the wee smug middle class twat, shocking him with my confessions, punching him to the ground and whatnot, it was a beautiful friendship and i started stalking the wee cunt, there was nothing else to do really during those endless orphan summer days, nothing much but baiting a wee middle class cunt and listening to manics songs.

THE VICIOUS WINE MERCHANT AND THE OBNOXIOUS OASIS FAN / i'm eating a mars bar and looking at my richey poster, the infamous pic, the one taken just after he carved '4real' on his arm, i used to do quite a bit of cutting carving and slicing myself but no one ever took a picture, tis a shame really cos it looked gorgeous: blood dripping on my white school blouse, on my jeans, blood smeared on the walls of the classroom, a trail of blood going from the bathroom to my bedroom to my father's office, blood smeared on my faded oasis posters, puddles, streams, torrents, my blouse soaked, fresh gaping wounds covering both my arms and i was so fucking beautiful back then, so fucking skinny, small and delicate, i was not fucked up then, i was not a drunkard; why, oh why, did they have to lock me up in the bloody mental asylum where i got slapped by jealous dykes, blackmailed by psychopaths, abducted by an albino junkie who wanted to sell me to a fat mustached italian businessman, patronised by bitchy nurses, betrayed by a baby-faced shrink, threatened by a psychotic ex-hooker, snogged by a demented toothless eighty year old lady, stabbed with a fork by a fifteen year old incest victim, grabbed at the throat by rita the compulsive cutter, courted by a paranoid ex-communist, an alcoholic reprobate, a jewish comedian with a tendency to jump off high buildings, a french bum who thought jim morrison's soul had moved into him, a silver haired illiterate ex-boxer, a morrocan dyke with a huge scar on her left cheek, a retarded flemish cook, a wild horny dark-haired orphan who thought i was "prettier than britney spears", a morrissey lookalike who wrote books about usa conspiracies against duran duran and the pet shop boys, a ruddy hairdresser who'd stabbed his sister to death (no, not with scissors), an autistic golf player who hid all blue objects and only wore red? and why, oh why, did i get raped by the sleazy nightnurse, and would my life be any different if i hadn't? possibly... but then maybe i was always destined to become an oasis obsessed slut with a drinking problem.

TINNED DEATH THREATS AND PLASTIC DOLPHINS / i wrote stories on the tinned meat yesterday at the godforsaken supermarket, they all went a little like this: "i hope you choke on these beautiful innocent heifers that were cruelly executed for your perverted needs, you rotten twisted middle class murderers, and if by any chance you don't choke or don't die of a stroke, you overfed bourgeois cunts, then i'll pay you a little visit, and i'll have my carving knife with me, and i'll festively slice all of you fucking appalling yuppie scum, you thought vegetarians were a bunch of silly harmless hippy fags, think again, bloody unimaginative barbarous bourgeois bastards, delphine", something in that vein, i showed my stories to peter peter jolly wife beater, a colleague i fancy, and he looked at me rather coldly and said "those aren't stories, those are death threats", and then the fucking arrogant cunt walked away and i threw my ladder at the smug cunt, but it missed him and it flew right into the face of a bespectacled corporate pig, his glasses landed on the floor where i "accidentally" crushed them with my trolley, the thick myopic corporate cunt narrowed his eyes and i poked my fingers into them, cos i thought there's no way this blind middle class wanker can see me, but i was wrong, typical corporate pig behaviour: pretending to be blind to get the sympathy of the people you exploit, pffffff, the corporate pig couldn't see the funny side of it and he grabbed my arm and dragged me into his office: "i'm a patient person, and i don't mind a little banter on the work floor, but you're pushing it, do you have any idea how much those glasses cost me?", "i'm guessing... TOO FUCKING MUCH, YOU LOADED OBNOX-

IOUS MIDDLE CLASS TWAT", "you're gonna have to apologise for this, young lady", "i was only trying to inject a little humour into the conversation", "is that your idea of humour, calling me a middle class twat?", "an obnoxious middle class twat, sir", "i don't find this amusing, i'm seriously considering giving you the sack", "by all means, sack me", "this is your last chance, do you hear me?", "that's what you said last time, and time before that", "i mean it this time, delphine, your last chance, now get back to work", i felt gutted, i didn't feel like stacking slaughtered heifers, so i walked out of the supermarket and roamed the streets, it was a bright day, i had my headphones on, i craved mischief and dodgy cock, i was frisking through piss-soaked alleys when i noticed a crouched figure sobbing in a pool of piss, spittle, spunk, blood-stained screwdrivers, used syringes and broken glass; it was christopher, my beloved rentboy with the beautiful straight indie hair and the big accusatory eyes, his nose was bleeding, he had a black eye, and his oasis t-shirt, the one i gave him for his birthday, was torn, beyond repair it bloody well was, i crouched down next to christopher, when i touched his shoulder he flinched, but when he saw it was only me he relaxed a little and i stroked his hair, even though there was dried-up blood, mucus and spunk sticking in it, "what's happened?", of course he wouldn't answer, so i took him to the zoo and we watched the zebras and counted their stripes and we tried to waggle like those funny penguins and we stared down lions and cobras and we upset the nocturnal animals by shining flashlights at them and we stole an asian otter and we liberated a few foxes and we threw tinned meat at the performing seals and i bought christopher a plastic dolphin that looked rather stupid and dull and then we had to run from the police, i suddenly remembered the asian otter in my backpack, we went to the supermarket and we left him on my boss's desk with a note saying "i hope this makes up for the broken glasses, fucking oversensitive myopic cunt, love, delphine", i then took christopher to my bedsit, he was rather cheerful now, me on the other hand, i was starting to feel all gloomy and angry, but i didn't show christopher, we listened to idlewild and christopher couldn't stop ranting about that skinny pedantic bookish roddy woomble wanker and his cute little nose and sultry hips and innocent eyes, "stop swooning, silly boy, he's a miserable indie poof and his songs are pish, you deserve better", "who do i deserve then?", "you deserve tim wheeler", "i do???", "of course you do, i wouldn't say so if you didn't", "do you remember when we visited him last time, he was proper pissed off with you", "ach, you know how fucking oversensitive these doe-eyed indie poofs are", but christopher wasn't listening any longer, he'd fallen asleep on the bed, i put a blanket over him and kissed his immaculate brow, retreated to my shower tray and called my sheffielder angel, we talked about dodgy britpop and football, i didn't mention tinned meat or the myopic corporate cunt cos i don't want him to know how fucking perverted some people are, heaven forbid i'd corrupt a sheffielder angel, after the phone call i wanked a little with my oilcloth knife, but my heart wasn't in it, i put on my headphones and the last thing i heard before i was at the mercy of the rotten twisted adults who populate my dreams was a sweet doe-eyed indie boy whispering "won't be saved".

SCRATCH MY NAME ON YOUR ARM WITH A RAZORBLADE / this train is taking me to the place where i was raised by my catholic alcoholic neurotic violent unpredictable grandparents, chirpy folks, no really, they used to give me some fair beatings but were always cheerful about it and they weren't vindictive; unlike my crazy, slutty, heavily made up teen mum who used to beat the shit out of me just for the sake of it, but backfire it did, and did i gloat? did i fuck? the bitch is in jail now for trying to rob a liquor store, hahaha, she miserably failed, the silly cow; my companion is ranting on about the third man... what the fuck??!! the third fucking man... go fuck yourself, pedantic little prick, go wank over an orson welles picture all you want, but let me drift away, let me sleep, dream, i'm gone, we pass hideous coastal towns, meadows, scorched earth, wasteland, container parks, sheds, cows, deer, crows, liam gallagher headbutting that slimy middle class blur geezer, morrissey gyrating and throwing daffodils at me, the family dog violently farting, the first time i saw the sea, the dunes ever so comforting, scavenging through school's constant lulls, soul mates, i had so many but i never told them that i have no soul, and now i'm cutting myself and the blood is dripping on the white blankets and i'm sure i'll never get out of this isolation cell, but then i'm at the front row of an r.e.m. gig and i'm singing but i got the words all wrong, it disnae matter love, and there he is now, michael stipe, utterly vain, shamelessly sexual, and i'm caressing his belly and all is bliss, the taxi takes me home but i've no money so i give the driver head instead, i'm lying on the freshly mown grass, the smell almost smothering me and i'm listening to the smiths, oh how i love my life; "sorry, i dozed off, do tell me about david lynch and roman polanski... hang on, isn't he the perv who got thrown out of the states for humping some under aged starlet... aye, i wanna hear about him".

MOST ALCOHOLIC SLAPPERS ARE / there are peacocks on my grandmother's curtains, but they look like vultures, their tails are ragged and faded and you can only make out their sharp beaks and their vile little eyes, i know that they're peacocks cos i bought the curtains with the old hag somewhere in the north of france fifteen years ago, we drove there in silence, we bought the curtains, we drove back in silence, we hung the bloody curtains, we stared at the peacocks and waited for my grandfather to come home; there are voracious birds everywhere actually, foul china swans on the mantelpiece, churlish sparrows on the box in which she keeps old keys, a minging rooster on her blue vase, even on her bottle of brandy there's a voracious grouse with bulging eyes and an eager razor-sharp beak, and of course her garden's infested with lairy magpies and lots of other obnoxious birds that i don't know the name of that can probably only survive in the old hag's garden; i'm here to settle old scores, i'm here to steal her savings and down her brandy- i'm here cos it's sunday and i'm bored out of my mind, wee andy's in dorset, christopher's in the arse of some perverted priest, and i can't think of too many other people i want to hang out with, i would hang out with the retarded flemish cook if he wasn't so damn broke, i would hang out with that sheffielder middle class cunt if he wasn't so damn dour, i would hang out with my dodgy neighbour if he wasn't so damn dodgy; i would hang out with a lot of people if they weren't so damn stingy, my grandmother's stingy sure enough, but at least i can rob her, she hasn't sewed her pouch to her groin like most stingy cunts i know, it's just lying on her bed, odd that she keeps a picture of my rotten twisted grandfather in her wallet, i thought she hated his guts, i bet she didn't keep it there when he was still alive, he's looking all smug and arrogant, pretending to be engrossed in some russian novel, pretending he's read it all before; i stuff the bank notes in my pockets, sit myself on the bed and start reading the old hag's diary, it's filled with rants about local cunts she fucks and fancies, it's poorly written, i throw it in the shrubs under her bedroom window, an explosion of mad chirping follows, i throw a russian novel out of the window just to hear it again, but it's not so violent this time, i look at my ghastly reflection in the window and punch it in the nose, an explosion of breaking glass follows, my hand's bleeding but the cuts aren't too deep, apparently i don't hate myself as much as i thought i did, i wash the splinters away and bandage my hand with one of the hag's silk scarves, i run out of the house, loaded and bleeding, though not really all that loaded, it's still very much sunday, fat germans are stuffing their faces with pancakes and crimson-coloured cocktails, seagulls are gnawing at orphan dolls, french kids are kicking a dead dog around, or maybe it's a cat, but if it's dead then why is it whimpering? i hide in a park but it's hardly a shelter, my bleeding fist attracts all the pervs, i ignore them but it's hard cos they're trying to unzip my jeans and they're rubbing my tits and i've only got one hand to defend myself with, i cling to the perv who looks the least perverted, he chases the others away and buys me a waffle and a stella in a seedy coastal pub that looks and smells like the hall of a disused flemish station, my chair is still warm from the person before me and i don't think i can ever get up again, the perv suggests we go upstairs to get to know each other better, oh these bloody euphemisms, i didn't even know this place had an upstairs, i get up and follow him, upstairs there are rooms with numbers on them, we go inside 212, it's ghastly, but probably not any ghastlier than the other rooms, at least there aren't voracious peacocks on the curtains, big ominous roses though, probably man-eating roses, and they have dodgy stains on their stems, they look a bit like daggers, the perv hates them as well cos he rips them out of the ceiling and throws them in the wee bathroom, he fucks me till my cunt's too sore to come, every five minutes or so a seagull collides with the window and drops dazed to the pavement, we both fall asleep around midnight, when i wake up i can't find the sink so i throw up on the curtains, the perv's still asleep, there's no breakfast downstairs, some hostile flemish bitch is mopping the floor, she unlocks the door, i step outside and the air's as rancid and uncompromising as it was yesterday.

CARESSING MICHAEL STIPE'S BELLY AND COUNTING FROZEN LOBSTERS / oh my god it just struck me: i'm never gonna swagger onstage, cool as fuck, stella in my left hand, the inevitable sunglasses, the charisma, the sex, blissfully ignorant, proud, arrogant, loutish, brash, rash, baiting a ten thousand crowd, fucking defiant and not just faking it, i'm never gonna be liam gallagher, how fucking tragic... my crowd consists of a vicious russian cow killer and a retarded flemish cook, how fucking tragic... i would rather not go back to the loony bin, i'm not going to spend my whole life in limbo, no, no, no; i loved the funny pills and the sleazy nurses and concocting all those stories of sexual abuse and rape, god i enjoyed that, and so did they, the hungry eager therapists practically driveling on their desk, give me more, tell me about that first night your father came to visit you, did you go down on him? did you swallow? did he penetrate you? are you hard yet, mr shrink? it was alright for a while but soon i wanted more, so i put off my straightjacket and moved in with this alcoholic ex-boxer who ranted tirelessly about past victories and all his childhood memories that were so long gone that they seemed to belong to someone else, of course this was doomed to fail, and we never even tried, we only clung to each other for a little while, i ran away, he drank himself into a coma and that was that and here i am, pissed but not defeated, angry but not sad; morrissey is watching me as i'm getting arsefucked by an old fat sleazy pub owner, looking at me with scorn and contempt, but when i study his face as i try not to come i notice a weak smile, weak but forgiving, and his eyes, they're not harsh, i was wrong, they radiate sympathy and comfort, and between the repulsive sighing and moaning of the aroused pig, i can hear morrissey whispering: "i know it's gonna happen someday", but then i come and morrissey's just a picture on my wall.

WEE ANDY WANTS TO GYRATE LIKE MORRISSEY / i'm sitting on my bedroom floor with wee andy, we're listening to liam, i'm marveling, wee andy's rolling his eyes like only wee andy rolls them; i call him "wee" andy yeah, it annoys the fuck out of him, he's not wee, he's taller than me, bigger, older, braver and possibly brighter, but aye, i have to call him wee andy cos he's so fucking sweet, almost innocent, and yes i want to shag him but i'd feel like a rapist so i'll just try to refrain and restrain and retire to the bathroom and wank over a cute picture wee andy once gave me, he probably doesn't know i still carry it with me, he's wearing a mickey mouse t-shirt in this picture (unironic! not like how those indie hipsters wear them), his thick brown hair freshly cut and washed, his big brown eyes glowing ever so friendly vividly, and his smile is broad though a little self-conscious, aaaah my wee andy how i want to straddle you and free you from the atrocious yoke of virginity; wee andy's written a song for me: "stay here", a plea to me to stay here, yeah wee andy's world is a simple one and it's also a beautiful and peaceful one where friends don't get raped, don't cut themselves and don't long for death, and he's singing it for me right now, it's pretty embarrassing, tis truly a dreadful song and i'm trying not to burst out in laughter, have to think horrible thoughts: tremendous fear of choking, my insomnia is getting worse, debts, am being stalked by a retarded flemish cook, i sell my body, i suck senior cock, i'm fox evil, i robbed my grandmother who's only just lost her husband, i refuse to feel guilty, all my friends are disloyal moody vile junkie scum, all my relatives are either hysterical spinsters or short-tempered sadists but all too often both, i'm trapped in these cruel cold streets and i'll probably never meet noel gallagher; but ach, wee andy's song is finished now and i'm crying, but only cos i know he'll try to comfort me, put his arms around me, gently caress my hair, put me on his lap, lull me, and whisper sweet words and dreary clichés into my ear.

COCK AND ICE CREAM IN BALTIMORE / some cocky editor from baltimore says i should fly over to suck his cock, i can even stay around for ice cream afterwards and hang around with his sister who's a whore and she's called gun and she's willing to refine my hooking skills, as if they need refining, if anyone will be teaching tricks it'll be me, baltimore does seem appealing, even if i've no idea where it is, it's in the states and morrissey's in the states, that should do, that would have done it if it wasn't for christopher, i found him on my doorstep last night, unconscious and with a heavily bleeding crotch, i carried him inside and laid him on the bed, i put on some sweet melancholic indie songs to soothe him: "would you turn off those whingeing indie poofs and put on some proper music?" i knew then that he'd be ok, so i put on some oasis and i felt a little awkward unzipping his pants despite all the blood, i did feel very aroused, he had a boner, it was severely cut, i kissed it and cleansed his wounds, christopher was groaning, "stop that, it's not the time nor erm the place", "i'm not coming for fuck's sake, i'm suffering", "fucking moody ungrateful slut", "oi", "shut up, rentboy", christopher tried to get up to punch me, but he was feeling too weak, "who did this to you?", "does it matter? it was a rotten twisted adult", "that's a little vague, that could mean anyone but us and morrissey", "and wee andy", "forget that insensitive middle class cunt, he's never gonna give up his smug comfortable middle class lifestyle to save us", "can you blame him?", "yes, i can and i will", "i want to sleep", "well you go to sleep then, fucking self-absorbed poof, just leave me at the mercy of abusive relatives with rifles and shovels...", "not this again", so i kissed him goodnight and faced the abusive relatives with rifles and shovels on my own, i wish i was in baltimore, the sun never sets in baltimore and there's always eager tanned cock and ice cream and cheerful hookers and cock-eyed poets, and morrissey's not that far, the fucking miserable poof breaks my heart every bleeding day, i need him so much, his songs just won't do, i need to smell him, i need to buy him christmas presents, does it even snow in l.a.? i fall asleep in my shower tray dreaming about dreary coastal towns, dolphins, jarvis cocker and my throbbing cunt being circumcised by a vindictive french porn star, i wake up and christopher's still sleeping, the bed is soaked with blood, he must have ripped off his bandages during his sleep, i put on some sweet melancholic indie songs, i don't care if the cunt opposes, i'll be fucking self-indulgent if i want, this song is so gorgeous, it's about days being uneventful, well that's a little hard to relate to, but such a heartrending melody, i can't take this anymore, "wake up, fucking shallow poof, wake up, wake up, i need you here", i bounce violently on the wounded slut, i pull at his beautiful straight indie hair and i pinch bite and slap him until he wakes up and throws me off him: "fucking crazy cunt, turn off those whingeing indie poofs", "christopher?", "WHAT???", "can i adopt you?", "oh bloody hell, i thought you wanted me to adopt you??!", "i did, but you cruelly rejected me", "no, i don't want to be adopted by some fucked up spiteful orphan girl WHO'S QUITE POSSIBLY YOUNGER AND MOST DEFINITELY CRAZIER THAN ME", "fucking ungrateful cunt, you can't just come lie on my doorstep wounded every bleeding night without expecting to be saved", "you can't save me, you're too fucked up", "harsh", "harsh but true", "i bloody well bandaged your fucking repulsive gaping festering crotch", "next time i'll go and lie on andy's doorstep", "yeah, you do that, just don't expect him to let you in, you don't seriously think the wee scared middle class cunt will let you ruin his carpet?! he'll just call an ambulance and you'll be locked in some ghastly nuthouse for a few years where you'll have to suck psychotic cock every day and at night you'll be brutally arsefucked by the sleazy nightnurse, but you'd love that, wouldn't you?" christopher just shrugs, he's put on the telly, it's children's television, some cartoon about an island full of suffering mammals, and there's one healthy kangaroo who tries to save all the rodents, dolphins, beetles, polar bears and gorillas until she gets fed up and decides to move to another place, but the polar bear fancies her and asks her to stay on the island, it's depressing, christopher reckons i'm a bit like that kangaroo, but i don't want to save anybody bar him, and no polar bear fancies me; christopher's crotch has started bleeding again, i disinfect it and refresh the bandages, we both cry a little after that, "i have absolutely nobody", "don't be so fucking pathetic, i have nobody either", "then why can't we help each other?", "it doesn't work that way", "how does it work then?", "we're whores, honey, we're on our own", "well that's a little depressing", christopher shrugs again, his eyes look so empty, drugged probably, totally indifferent definitely, i go out to buy us some breakfast, when i get back, the fucking unfaithful rentboy's gone, all he's left is a blood-soaked bed and a few crumpled bank notes.

NO STRINGS AND NO FLIES / i am running to my sheffielder angel's place, i am running cos i'm so eager to tell him about my latest religious experience, even if i know he's gonna laugh cynically and tell me to cut down on the booze, cos god only visits stuck-up sheffielder middle class cunts don't you know? why would he visit a minging whore who's determined to destroy her life and make twenty kinky flemish fishmongers' lives hell whilst at it? and i can't answer that, maybe he's fed up with boring overprivileged sheffielder yuppie cunts who only ever pray for promotion or scottish minge? how the fuck should i know? i'm not even supposed to believe in god; i enter a small dusty supermarket and buy a bottle of bourbon and chestnuts and fags and a smoked peacock, i shoplift a frozen lobster and a comb; i sit myself in front of the disused court house and smoke a few fags, a dour german hobo comes sitting next to me, i ask him if he wants to hear about my religious experience, he says "no", i ask him if he wants to hear about my religious experience whilst sharing this bottle of expensive bourbon with me, he still says no, i get up and start running again, the jars in my bags are clanging so loudly i have to stop running cos everyone's looking at me and i hate it when everyone's looking at me and scoffing at my ungracious clumsy ways, i drop the bags and hide inside a telephone booth, i call wee andy: "andy, something amazing happened, i just had to tell you", "please tell me it isn't another one of your religious experiences?!", "as a matter of fact, it is, i met HIM in the seedy arcade last night, i was sitting on the doorstep of the closed video shop, a cancerous alsatian pissed at my feet, i was slightly annoyed cos some of it spattered my brand new sneakers, but then the pool of piss started talking to me!!!!!", "god?", "yes, god himself, and last night he had a husky woman's voice, i was quite aroused to be honest, she sounded so hot", "what did god tell you?" but then the line goes dead and i haven't got any coins left to tell wee andy what god told me, it doesn't matter, he doesn't give a fuck anyway, that bloody heathen jock; i'm running again, i stop at a stall that sells musty french crime novels, i buy one for my sheffielder angel, of course he doesn't understand french, but he can always jerk off to the cover cos there's a picture of a lecherous slavonic bitch on it and she's playing with herself, feigning ecstasy, oozing boredom and a deep-seated hatred for everything west european; i'm standing in front of my sheffielder angel's smug building, all of a sudden i dread going inside, i decide not to, that self-complacent bourgeois cunt hates my guts anyway, and i hate his; i give the french crime novel to a minging russian hobo who's sitting on a piss-soaked bench in front of the sinister post office, i sit myself next to him and take the frozen lobster from under my sweater, it's hardly thawed, but we eat it anyway, i use the stolen comb to crack its spine and pick out the soft bits, i stuff the lobster's claws in the back pocket of my jeans and walk back to my sheffielder angel's place; i stop the elevator between the second and the third floor and jab my minge with the lobster's claws, i zip up my jeans and take the elevator to the tenth floor, and then back to the third floor, i get out and knock on my sheffielder angel's door, he lets me in, pours me a pint of liverpudlian cider, i down it and ask if i can use his telephone, i call wee andy: "andy, it's me again, i'm sorry about earlier, i'd run out of small change", "that's ok... so what did god tell you?", "he told me that i should stop shoplifting frozen lobsters!! and guess what i did today", "you shoplifted a frozen lobster?", "exactly!", "aren't you afraid he's gonna punish you?" my sheffielder angel is leaning on me, he's blowing hot air into my right ear, "look, andy, i have to go, my sheffielder angel is blowing hot air into my right ear, i think he wants another blowjob", "aye, take care mate, catch you later", "bye"; i hang up, unzip my sheffielder angel's pants and suck his cock, i catch his cum in my palm, i kinda expect it to talk to me, but it's cold and sticky and mute.

DISCIPLINE,CONTRITION,BOREDOM,OX / i am reading wee andy's palm: "you will be trampled by an equine creature in april, it's hard to read when exactly, you have a very messy palm", "will anything exciting happen to me before i die?" the wee cynical cunt says all coolly mockingly, "hmm, there's a minging orphan girl who will spraypaint slanderous stories on your bedroom walls on the fourth of march, you will also be attacked by a mancunian shepherd at the end of march!", "there are no shepherds in manchester", i read his palm more carefully, "it's illegible, i'm sorry, but what i can make out is that he's gonna shove five frozen hesperian hares up your bony arse", "oh shut up", "don't shoot the messenger, andy", wee andy rolls his eyes and gets up, he leaves the kitchen, oh well, i'll have to read my own palm: eww, that's just disgusting, oh no, that's horrible, so many?? but that's physically impossible, twenty mongolian longbows in one hour, oh dear, a stand-up comedian from milwaukee? my sheffielder angel's gonna let me suck his endearingly black cock on the 26th of february, a car accident, will i limp? another crack-crazed badger, 22 polish gynaecologists... wee andy's back, "maybe this'll make you feel better", i show him my palm, "oh i forgot: you can't read palms... it's fucking miserable, lots of wax and stuffed rodents, lots of kinky clerics, lots of treacherous middle class twats, lots of stitches, lots of blood, BUT: i get to fondle my sheffielder angel's cock on the 26th of february!!", "that's great", we put on our coats and scarves and leave the house, we walk into the wee forest next to the disused russian casino where i danced on green velvet and sold my good luck to a gullible liverpudlian jockey one sultry summer night two years ago, we sit ourselves on the mossy paws of a bronze satyr, satyrs aren't supposed to look this gloomy and self-conscious, i spit on his bronze knee and light a cigarette, "discipline", "what??", "can't a girl say random words out loud??", "i suppose she can", a ruddy conceited tourist passes, i scowl and hiss at him, "contrition", wee andy sighs and kicks leaves, "boredom", "despair?", "no, no, not despair, guilt perhaps? or maybe something a bit more crass: ox", "discipline, contrition, boredom, ox??", "and why the hell not?" the wee dour middle class cunt shrugs, "damnation", "oh shut up", "damnation! i've accidentally swallowed the key to my dodgy neighbour's safe, the one where he keeps my lithium and my tacky bracelets and the key to my handcuffs, he's gonna beat me to death", the wee endearing twat starts stroking my hair, "blimy", "now what?", "we're back in the game, thick cunt", "maybe i don't like your game", "don't be so bloody childish", "starvation", "that's no good, you lose, i get to pick two words", "that's so unfair", "bereavement, donkey", "appetite", "pattern", "lovelorn", "don't be such a poof", "what's wrong with lovelorn??", "too fucking sentimental... i get to pick two words: edelweiss, incest", "poverty", "are you trying to depress me?", "what's so cheerful about your words? bereavement, incest, boredom...", "alright, alright, you can have your poverty... punctuation", "goldfish", "tenant", "apology", "pffffff, i'm fed up with your silly game", "it's your game", i bite wee andy's hand angrily playfully and run out of the wee forest, how dare he diss my game, that wee arrogant cunt, i can't wait to attend his funeral in april, i sit myself on the doorstep of a closed irish grocery and wait for the illiterate rentboy, i wait till the sun starts setting, he's probably dead, strangled by some perverted vicar, bless him, the rentboy, not the vicar, "i'm sorry i'm late, i had to jerk off that vicious cuban vicar, he bloody well nearly strangled me", thank god he's alive, he sits himself next to me, we share a bottle of spanish rum, i tell him about the game, he doesn't get it, i don't get it either, "orifice", "moon", "redemption", "fringe", "hey! you are good at the game! much better than that wee jock, he's way too well-read to be good at the game... statistics", "navy", we play the game till two am and then we go back to more violent games, the ones wee andy refuses to play: mugging self-complacent middle class cunts and selling our supposedly underage chests to rotten twisted locals.

LIVING IN A SHOWER TRAY / i'm sitting in my shower tray, since christopher's been resting in my bed i sleep here, to be completely honest i already slept here before christopher occupied my bed, i like it here, it smells of soap and spunk, it's a small bathroom and it doesn't quite smother the drunken brawls and whimpering junkies, but it does make them sound all muffled and deformed, and sometimes the threats kinda echo and bounce against the walls, but it's not frightening, it's amusing, i feel safe, the shower tray is also where i have my nightly telephone conversations with my sheffielder angel, in the daytime he takes off his wings and disguises himself as a corporate pig but at night he turns into this wonderful creature who heals the crippled, comforts the lonely, and encourages the warped; i am crippled as well as lonely as well as warped, which means i get three times the attention most souls get; the shower tray is also where i wank, recently i've discovered that wanking with my fingers can be almost as satisfying as wanking with garden rakes, but no not really, it's just that my garden rake doesn't fit in my bathroom; i always wank when i talk to my sheffielder angel, and i tell him but it doesn't affect him or our relationship, typical me though, trying to corrupt an angel; i write lots of daft poetry in my shower tray and then i gleefully watch the sleazy sentences blur into one as i turn on the tap until they're nothing but pulp and they disappear down the drain, and what a fucking relief, heaven forbid my beloved relatives would read all those poems about throbbing cunts and crooked cocks, and crooked cocks massacring throbbing cunts, and rotten twisted adults shoving their callous fingers into orphan cunts, and all that vulgar inappropriate stuff people should never write about, at least not with such relish; why would i ever leave the house again? i'm perfectly happy in my shower tray, and if i want cock, i invite some perv to my shower tray and he slams my head against the tiles, forces me to eat the dead hair that's blocking the drain, shoves the douche up my arse and turns the tap on and it's such an explosive cum that i always pass out, and if it wasn't for christopher i'd choke to death, but at least i'd die with a ferociously throbbing cunt and fresh spunk and blood trickling down my face, and wouldn't that just be the most glorious death ever? it's a shame one can't choose their persecutors though, some of these pervs are well dodgy, and i'd rather be executed by someone a little brighter and sexier, i know how shallow this must sound, but fuck it, murder is serious business and it's a bloody shame that it's available to all these unimaginative bastards nowadays; the snippets of conversation i catch are rather depressing, incest and prostitution seem to be recurring themes, maybe i'm talking to myself, or maybe my neighbours are talking to themselves, or maybe they're talking about me? is it written all over my face? it bloody well isn't, i walk and talk proud, i don't fucking cower, i don't cringe, i don't flinch, and i can stare down any rotten twisted adult, bar my mother; christopher has made me strong just by letting me lull him to sleep, sometimes life can be that simple, sometimes christopher has to restrain pervs who slam my head against the tiles too eagerly, sometimes he has to throw them out, the tiles are smeared with blood and shit and ink and spunk, it doesn't keep the pervs away, quite the opposite, slashing my face with tweezers until i'm nothing but scar tissue and two big scared eyes doesn't keep them away either, it never works that way, sometimes christopher calls me a sad ugly fucked up slut, the pot calling the kettle black indeed, except christopher is gorgeous, which increases his chances of being adopted by some old bored lonely loaded tart, i told him this, he laughed and shrugged: "why would i want to be adopted by some old bored lonely loaded tart, when i'm already adopted by a sweet considerate orphan girl?" and when he says "sweet considerate orphan girl", he's referring to me.

LIFE'S A ZOO / i'm very hungover today, it's total bliss, i feel gorgeous and brilliant, i'm not like all those sad alcoholic fucks who feel guilty and depressed and scared and whatnot when they're hungover, i laugh in their faces, i laugh at their sorry lives and their stupid excuses and their silly wish to escape, to start again, bah, they're no proper drunkards, i am the real deal: i shagged a seventy-three year old perv last night, we downed four bottles of wine and i woke up in my own vomit and i'd shat myself, i woke up smiling and whistling oasis songs, "if you ever need a cum just come to me", that's what he said, that's what i did last night, i went to my old deluded neighbour, i even dressed up for the old fart: my fanciest lingerie, red and lace, nice miniskirt, tight black blouse, tits well pronounced, nipples well hard, he could not keep his hands off me, which was nice, i was only just seated next to him in the couch when he started caressing my thighs and running a finger round my nipples and then we downed a few glasses of wine and he got bolder, he pushed up my skirt and gently fingered me, i was gagging for it, fuck me, lick me, destroy me; it got darker, we got even more drunk, he put a few cushions under my arse so that my cunt was facing him and he licked it for hours on end, i came once twice many times silently screaming sighing groaning grinding moaning crying yelling sweating inundating the living room with all my juices, and all the while dave gahan was twisting his bare-chested body on stage, singing his heart out for me, i was so glad he was there when i came.

I KNOW A STATION WHERE THE SUN HITS THE SKY / i'm feeling really sorry for myself, i'm sitting on a bench in the coldest and the most ghastly station in the world, it's late, it's cold, it's january, its my birthday and the station is completely deserted, i'm wearing jeans and an oasis t-shirt, i lost my shoes whilst escaping from another bloody rapist and i don't care if you wank in them, you rotten twisted adult, and if you do wank in them i hope your cock will catch some very persistent warts and that'll teach you, thank god i grabbed my walkman when running away from there, i even smacked him in the face with it, i can't say he was very impressed, the fat bourgeois cunt ran after me for hours, over frozen meadows, total fucking wasteland, no houses, no people, only this heavily breathing rapist and the cracks of the frozen soil, i was scared, i'll admit to that much, i was scared cos he seemed so fucking determined, and most rapists- as cruel and aggressive as they may be- are not willing to run after a skinny minger for hours on end in the freezing cold, they'll mutilate the minge when it's within range, but if you somehow miraculously escape, well then that's it, and that's luck for you; but this bastard, he sure is the tenacious type, of course not half as tenacious as someone who's afraid to lose her life, that's why i'll always win, the rapist merely wants some minge to massacre, but i want to live this wonderful life and there's so much that still needs to be done, said and written, so much revenge, so many stories, so many indie gems that yet remain undiscovered, and there's still so many people who think i loathe them when really i'm madly in love with them and it's about time i told them, and i desperately need to see oasis live again, and i haven't trashed enough churches yet, and i still haven't found out how to graciously gyrate like morrissey, and i've never even been to manchester, and there's still so much i have to confess to my sheffielder angel, and there are still so many unscathed areas on my body that need to be slashed and scarred, and i want to punch my mother right in her vile cold face and i want my fist to be specked with her blood, all those songs i have to learn by heart, all those nights i have to get pissed and maudlin and wank with my toggled hand harpoon while nicky wire is getting it on with richey, and i have to find richey, and i want to hear jarvis whisper "good god" at least a thousand more times cos it sounds so gorgeously guttural when he says it and it makes my cunt throb so insanely that i always fall from my bike when i have that song on my walkman, so many wounded pigeons and trembling orphan boys that need to be saved, so many pervs that need to be obliterated, so many frightening letters i still have to send to liam and noel, and i just know that morrissey's gonna welcome me with open arms when i finally make it to his doorstep and he will buy me a depressed goldfish with big accusatory eyes and black jumpers and a sleigh, and he will tuck me in ever so fatherly, and i will spend christmas with him and he will wear the red scarf i knitted for him, and i'm sure that the spiteful busker will read my stories if i point a gun to his head, and i want to turn christopher back into the sweet boy he used to be and convince him that he needs a mother rather than a nefarious pimp and i want to be that mother and i think he should sob in my arms rather than in the lap of some perverted vicar, oh i even want to hear wee andy yodel like an arctic fox that's being clubbed to death cos for all his spineless poof ways and his fucking happy untroubled childhood he's still the most endearing person i know and the only person who understands that i sometimes have to tie gag assault harass bait stalk and slander him and that it's my warped way of telling him how much i love him and he never holds it against me, he just shakes his head wearily, and if i don't make it home tonight i'll never see that oasis documentary and i'll never get to explain to my sheffielder angel just how witty noel is and how he slagged liam off, but it wasn't harsh and cold, it was brotherly, and i wish noel was my brother, he'd protect me against dodgy people and i'd never get raped and i'd never have to run for my life, barefooted, on this frozen ground, pursued by a vicious vindictive rotten twisted adult whose tenacity i might have underestimated, and where the hell have all the houses gone?? and all the streets?? and all the lights?? and where are all the people?? are we the only two people left in this rotten wonderful world?? and who will win if we finally fight it out?? the fearless minger or the loveless rapist?? i put my money on the fearless minger; a street at last! cars cars cars!!! HEADLIGHTS, and i jump in front of a speeding car and it brakes violently and swerves, i jump in the car and the lady chauffeur looks a little bemused, shocked really, i lock the doors, the rapist's gone, the lady smells nice, she's wearing beautiful earrings and i think she's well fit, we just drive around for a bit, we don't talk, she puts on the radio and supergrass are singing about a place where the sun hits

the sky and i ask the nice lady if she can take me there, "how about the station?" she rather cynically retorts, and i suppose the station is as close as i'll ever get to a place where the sun hits the sky; so that's how i ended up in this dreary station where the sun doesn't really hit the sky, but then it's almost midnight and i'm sure that
things will look so much brighter in the morning.

NOT VULGAR ENOUGH / i'm reading flemish bedtime stories to the perv's kids, yes, most pervs have got kids, why pick up random minging slappers from the streets if you can spawn your own minging slappers?! i can tell by their cynical comments and the scars on their swollen bellies that they're being subjected to impatient cock and eager fists every bleeding day, but i'm not gonna try to save them, the girl's eight and the boy's ten, which means that they're fucked up beyond repair and no amount of coffee flavoured lollipops and oasis songs can save them now, i should know; after he's fucked and tucked in his kids, the perv fetches a bottle of red wine from his well-used cellar, at least he doesn't say much, i know the names of his kids but i don't know his, i'm sure it's something long and ominous and guttural, and i'm sure it means "he who chats up minging slappers in seedy coastal pubs, lures them to his place with morrissey quotes and bank notes and tries to rape them in front of his kids", admittedly he didn't try to rape me, how can i be raped if i never say no? he paints the façades of nuthouses for a living, he baits them nutters by flashing his repulsive cock at them and slipping his twisted tales through the bars and grilles, and if the content of the stories isn't enough to make them sick of the outside world for the rest of their lives, there's always some kinky nightnurse who'll find the stories and act on them; he's reading me one of his stories right now, but i can't hear him cos i'm listening to his traumatised emaciated children who are crying and trembling so hard the whole house is shaking, but actually it's cos there are randy cats in the piss-soaked alley nearby, and i'm the one trembling, not cos i'm scared but cos his cold hands are stroking my spine and it feels a bit like there are two vile baby alligators crawling up and down my back, not that that's ever happened to me in real life, but in my dreams it happens all the time, yesterday i dozed off in my shower tray, this was just after the retarded flemish cook had tried to smother me with all his sickening presents and all his poisonous drivel, i dreamt that my shower tray was a teeming swamp of little red snakes and mean baby alligators who crawled up and down my back and lashed me with their callous tails, when i woke up i was choking on all the red slutty knickers the retarded flemish cook buys me every bleeding day, and christopher was lashing me with an altar cloth, like all illiterate rentboys he bites the hand that feeds him, and i can't blame them, if there was a hand feeding me i'd wolf it down and puke it out and wouldn't feel the least bit guilty about it; when he arsefucks me i think about the nice things christopher thinks about when he's being arsefucked by perverted priests, but the performing seals and crippled alsatians are only making me sadder, when the church bells chime he cums on my back and spits in my face, it's midnight and he's got no time for a slapper who retches when he cums in her mouth and flinches when he punches her in the nose and who wouldn't recognise a great story if it battered her face with a crowbar, he shoves a tenner in my knickers and kicks me out; i'm roaming the cruel coastal alleys, everywhere seagulls with deformed beaks are picking on emaciated orphan boys, the perv's daughter was nothing like me, i never wore my wounds with pride, i have to parade them into people's faces all the time, and the only people who don't back away repelled are pervs eager to add a few wounds, fellow whores don't back away either, they just don't give a fuck; my favourite fellow whore is christopher, and i'm glad when i bump into him in the piss-soaked alley where we always used to sniff glue and draw fatally wounded cubs on the walls, we don't have the time to do those things now, we're too busy dodging vindictive johns and affectionate alsatians, i get tired sometimes, we're hiding behind a blood-stained mattress in a deserted car park, the car park belongs to the supermarket where i stack dolphin safe tuna and shag lecherous butchers between all those frozen heifers, so bloody frozen that i can't imagine them frisking around in those bleak flemish meadows; we're drinking dark tepid beer that smells of burnt tires and christopher's hair, when he comes home from one of his perverted vicars, blood-soaked and bawling; i tell the illiterate rentboy about all the avenging beasts i dodged on my way to him, and where's that bass coming from? it's in my head apparently, every time i take a swig from the beer it triples, i guess it's always better than having thirty emaciated orphans in your head who are pleading with their sleazy guardians not to tuck them in; four hours before the sun comes up, the supermarket starts buzzing and rattling, neon lights are scoffing at our greasy hair and sickly skin, we run away from that wretched lair and hide inside an empty bus station, there's a love letter lying on the sticky floor, christopher asks me to read it to him, but i can't, it's too vulgar.

FAMILIARLY RED / "why bother calling me if you're gonna be gruff, wee strange bastard?", "i just wanted to make sure you're ok", "well i haven't jumped off a high building yet", "good", "no, it's not good, silly optimistic middle class cunt, by the way i'm slashing my groin with a chisel as we speak", "no you're not", "let's go to the zoo today", "there's no way i'm ever going to the zoo with you again", "why not?", "those crocodiles bloody well nearly devoured me", "you're such a drama queen... let's go to the cinema", "there's no way i'm ever going to the cinema with you again", "why not?", "you bloody well know why not", "because i set the screen on fire?", "well yes", "i hated that villain", "he wasn't for real, it's called acting", "smart cunt... let's go to the museum together, no wait, i already know the answer: there's no way i'm going to the museum with you ever again", "no actually the museum seems like a good idea", "wee contrary bastard", "which museum though?", "you pick one, you're the middle class cunt", "ask christopher to come along", "rentboys don't go to museums", "those are stereotypes, delphine", "yeah, what are you gonna do about it, bloody unimaginative middle class cunt?" wee andy's sighing, "hey, can you hear the music?", "what music?", "the music in the background, wee thick cunt... wait", i put the phone against one of the boxes, "i don't recognise it, what is it?", "it's so obscure that it hasn't even got a name", "very funny", "yes", "no seriously, what is it?", "i'm not telling", "fuck you, i don't wanna know anyway, i was just being friendly", "shut up, wee short-tempered cunt", "you're one to speak", "stop baiting me, wee nasty cunt", "i'll pick you up in an hour", "no, i'll pick YOU up in an hour", "fine", "dandy", and i break the connection, the wee cunt is getting a bit cheeky, it does worry me; christopher is fast asleep, his body's covered in liam pics, i sit next to him for a few minutes, he looks anxious and tormented like all rentboys look when they're sleeping, i hope i don't look like that when i sleep, i stroke christopher's hair which seems to make him even more anxious and tormented, pffff, i'm fucking useless at comforting rentboys, i'm pissed off with myself, and with the world at large, pissed off with myself cos i can't save christopher, pissed off with the world at large cos they fucked christopher up in the first place; wee andy's waiting for me on his doorstep, "aren't you gonna invite me in?", "erm, the place is a bit of a mess", but i kick the front door open and go inside: "seems fine by me, you wee inhospitable cunt... oh you bought new furniture, and its just as atrociously tacky as the old stuff", "well i bloody well had to buy new furniture after you smeared the old stuff with your blood and shit and whatnot", "you didn't have to buy atrocious furniture though, did you?", "i happen to like my new furniture", "you happen to be a wee thick unimaginative bourgeois cunt with no taste whatsoever", "cheers, mate", "i'm so tired andy, can i sleep in your bed?", "i thought we were going to the museum", "do you really think i want to waste a whole afternoon staring at pretentious mediocre concept bollocks made by pretentious little over-privileged middle class twats??!", "but it was your idea", "no, it wasn't, you wee bloody lying scum", wee andy's rolling his eyes, "ok, i need to sleep or i'm gonna die, and wouldn't that be a terrible loss?!" wee andy's still rolling his eyes, "play me some of your sleep-inducing indie ballads", i'm lying in andy's bed, the wee miserable poof is sitting on the bedroom floor strumming his guitar, whining and whimpering, although he insists on calling it singing, the wee sentimental cunt has actually made a song about me, its highly embarrassing so i put the blanket over my head, it doesn't completely drown the sound, i can still hear all the silly middle class platitudes and the supposed concern and the contrived tenderness, i'm trying not to be touched, i'm finding it very easy, i do feel mellow, but it's nothing to do with the wee cunt's silly songs, its just that i feel so good in his bed, safe really, and i hate myself for letting off my guard, and i hate wee andy for being so nice and forgiving, so i pull out my chisel and stab myself in my belly, the immaculately white sheets turn familiarly red.

DADDY DOESN'T LIKE CHEAP CHAT / the only thing i have in common with my father is that we both hate my mother; the man sitting across from me at the kitchen table is probably my father, although he looks nothing like me he's just as spiteful and vindictive, he's a beautiful man, i'd shag him, he's got thick dark hair, dark skin and a slender body, nothing like this here miserable dwarf, and we're drinking wine, and we're listening to the beatles (how can someone so spiteful love the beatles? oh yes, i forgot: charles manson), and we're not talking, and we're not looking at each other... "liam looks like a monkey", well it's a start, though i wish he'd said something more sensible... "ach dad, oasis are ten times more adventurous than the beatles"... and the thick cunt takes the bait, he gets all wound up, face reddening, moustache trembling, his knuckles stark white, i've got my little superior scornful smile on my face and i'm rolling my eyes from time to time, i'm rapping my knuckles on the table, and i'm whistling an oasis song, come on, why don't you hit me, i know you want to, after all i'm the wench's spawn, but it's me who lashes out, a mighty slap, it seems to echo for an eternity until it stops abruptly and i'm holding my arms in front of my face, fending off a furious blow, but my father just stands up, looks at my liam posters and says: "he does look like a monkey though".

IAN BROWN AND THE LOGBOOK OF MY WOUNDS / i'm walking to the bloody supermarket, there are birds singing in the trees and i want to throw sticks and stones at them, i hate them so much, and there is an old dodgy cunt cleaning his windows and i hate him as well, and i scowl at all the passing cars and i hate them so much, i can't stop crying, i'm listening to my mix tape and all the songs are so fucking sad, even the jaunty britpop songs, and i hate them cos they won't comfort me, they are just scoffing at me because i feel so fucking sorry for myself, i'm pathetic, i want to kill myself but i'm too tired to throw myself in front of the speeding vehicles, and there are no speeding vehicles anyway cos it's five am and the streets are deserted, i am completely alone, like i've never been alone before and i do not like it, cock would do me a world of good i'm thinking, but there is no cock in sight, there are milk bottles that need stacking, i spent the whole night throwing abuse at my sheffielder angel cos he'll just reject me like all those other rotten twisted adults, and i love him too much, and if he doesn't want to adopt me then his friendship is useless to me anyway, you lot are all insensitive middle class bastards, don't fucking gloat, save me shag me adopt me, i'm not a bleeding writer, i'm an orphan, well sod the lot of you, i don't need you anyway, i've got ian brown and he never lets me down, and he's wild, and he's dangerous, and he's got big girly eyes and a gorgeous fringe, and when he sings about cold and lonely streets i want to die; i have absolutely nothing, and i want to slaughter all middle class cunts who've had a happy childhood, and i want to slaughter all the fucked up orphan girls who moan about their miserable childhood, i hate you all, there's nothing left inside me now but spite, i should stop crying cos i'm at the supermarket now: horrible neon lights, smudged aprons, vulgar patter, tinned meat, corporate pigs calling me a lazy slag, cheap sentimental flemish ballads, people getting sacked, cowering unions, the stench of murder, the greedy sleazy customers, pallets reaching the ceiling, looted shelves, my sorry wage, loud ugly ads praising loud ugly products, backstabbing cunts counting frozen lobsters, glass jars bigger than my hands, clocking in, clocking out, overtime, being chatted up by kinky merchants, lying on my belly to stack dead animals on the bottom shelf, being humiliated by a middle class cunt who's never heard of ian brown, broken trolleys, throwing away stale food, standing on my ladder seeing nothing but tortured heifers in cans jars tins packets and bottles, broken discoloured hair roots, shabby lockers, sad dreary canteen, the prospect of unemployment, fucking depressing, all of it; but then it's over cos i'm free and wild and sexy, and i get lots of cock, and there's a gorgeous picture of ian brown on my wall; i cut the palm of my hand with my stanley knife, the blood is trickling down my filthy apron and jeans onto the ugly soiled infected supermarket floor, people are panicking, the sweet gorgeous blond girl who stacks the candy is stroking my hair and telling me that it's gonna be alright, i get carried upstairs by the very fatherly wine bottle stacker, rudiger, he's german and austere, he carries me to the infirmary, i rest my head on his broad shoulder, he lies me down on a white table which i immediately smear with my blood, i only cut myself cos i knew rudiger would take care of my wound, he cleanses my wounds so tenderly, he scolds me when i pick at the disinfected wound, i don't ever wanna leave this room, after my hand is bandaged my german saviour has to write down in a logbook where the accident happened, how bad it was, who witnessed it, who cleansed the wounds etc etc, the logbook is full of my wounds and rudiger cleansing them.

TWO WHORES CAN PLAY AT A DIFFERENT GAME / wee andy is silently zealously ironing his white shirt, it's a sunny coastal day, the kind of day that drives gloomy people who sometimes hear accusatory flemish voices in their heads to taking double doses of lithium and to bludgeoning their dodgy neighbour's cattle and/or wife to death, wee andy is too fucking endearing for his own good, does he expect some kind of reward in his next life? a less fucked up best friend? an equine reincarnation? better hair? more talents? a sturdier bone structure? a mightier cock? maybe there is no afterlife at all, but i hope for his sake that there is: such a dreary corporate existence, and i hope for my sake that there is: such violent whoring bondage, maybe the afterlife is just more violent whoring bondage, but without oasis and without the illiterate rentboy and without pencils to dash down the misery and without walls to dash it down on, "it doesn't bear thinking", "what doesn't?", "capital punishment, it just doesn't bear thinking, and also: i really dread going to my neighbour this afternoon and having to tell him about all my sleazy stepfathers and their incestuously elaborate ways whilst he's poking my minge with a japanese longbow", "well at least he doesn't use arrows", "fuck you, smart cunt", i leave wee andy's house and comb the coastal arcades for the only rentboy i want to share my afterlife with, he's taking guilty swigs from a bottle of cheap greek geneva on the doorstep of a disused tattoo parlour, i snatch the bottle and fling it at a fibre elephant that will blow a beatles song if you put coins in its trunk, sod the beatles, "come outside and play with me", "play at what?", "hide from our repulsive middle-aged johns in the deserted car park of the closed polish wheelbarrow factory and seek comfort in sniffing glue and stroking crippled alsatians", "ok", we leave the arcade and mournfully apathetically trudge to the car park, i: mournfully, christopher: both mournfully and apathetically, i have to drag him for miles, and now he's just standing still and refusing to budge, like some desperate bovine creature on its way to the slaughter-house, "if you're gonna do your mute traumatised retarded rentboy bit for the whole afternoon then that's fine by me but i'm not gonna stay here to watch it, it's just not entertaining enough and i've promised the kinky flemish fishmonger who lives in that lugubrious cottage opposite that sinister abbey where you once got raped by a stout mancunian playwright that i'd jerk him off for five codlings at three... i've half a mind to kick your shins and to spit on your nape and to call you names, you know", "he was from liverpool, not manchester", we resume our mournful and apathetic trudge, "it doesn't bear thinking", "what doesn't bear thinking?", "life without wee andy", "is he moving??", "i don't know, he tells me fuck all, i don't give a fuck about that dour self-important twat, he can move to anchorage for all i care, he can die of skin cancer for all i care, good riddance it'd be", "but i thought you loved him", "don't be so bloody sentimental, christopher", we enter the car park and sit ourselves in a rusty volvo that's missing its hind wheels, "a whore is like the icing on your pervy uncle's birthday cake/ she tastes so sweet but her empathy is fake..", "OH BLOODY HELL, not those silly rhymes again", "a whore is like a confessional box in a dreary empty church/ you fill her orifices with cross-bows and secrets and spunk, and then homewards you lurch/ a whore is like an ominous alley you have to go through to reach your corporate job/ she is quite minging, even a little bit scary, but at least she knows how to use her gob/ a whore is like a fibre elephant in a seedy coastal arcade/ you roll your eyes at so much cheapness, then you grab it tightly and never notice it fade/ a whore is like the wee stain on your immaculate smart tie/ rub her as harshly as you want, she won't die/ a whore is like a mouthful of chicken that goes wrong/ she won't stick around to save some repulsive john...", "they're getting awful now", we get out of the volvo and play at sniffing glue and setting a minging russian hobo on fire and selling our battered genitals to perverted austrian priests.

COME EDEN,COME EDEN,COME / i'm sitting on my doorstep enjoying the sun, i'm in one of my rare romantic moods, i'm surrounded by three orphan kittens, i'm listening to morrissey, i'm staring down cocky mancunian tourists, my cunt is throbbing, i'm scribbling down nonsense in my new notebook, just a few silly poems about short-tempered kangaroos and lovelorn ponies, this is my empire, i can be as self-indulgent as i want and i'm not about to restrain myself, i'm feeling quite happy, there's no sharp implement in sight, i'm not in love, i'm not especially craving cock, nor conversation; the supermarket has evaporated and my past no longer haunts me, sure i still hate the cunt that spawned me, but i don't want to kick her head in, she'll suffer more growing old anyway; all my other relatives i don't ever want to see again, but i love them, about as much as i love the grocer; who should come and disturb my eden- it sounds pompous, but if morrissey's there and creative juices are flowing on a puke-stained doorstep whilst three orphan kittens are rubbing their wet snouts in my face, then that's the first word that comes to mind- if it isn't the ever so repulsive ex-wine merchant, the old racist pig, the sleazy silver-haired archer, my dodgy neighbour, he's inviting me to his place for a quick drink, "will there be sex involved?", "probably", "good", and bang, eden explodes, and right on time i should add, cos i was getting a little bored on my puke-stained doorstep, and the creative juices are but measly drops compared to the juices that are constantly flowing from my throbbing cunt; my kinky neighbour's living room looks homelier every time i come back, and i always come back eventually; it used to be a ghastly murky room where i got arsefucked with toggled hand harpoons whilst old dour flemish women were looking down on me with contempt and gloating as i was tied to the radiator stark naked and bleeding; now it's a snug colourful room where i get arsefucked with paring gouges whilst i look up at old dour flemish women with defiance gloating as i think of the cruel deaths they died and the uneventful lives they led, they only ever had one cock, which they had to share with about a hundred other women; we watch the telly and down two bottles of red wine, i straddle my neighbour and hump his leg, he rips off my clothes and throws me on the table, he eats my cunt for hours on end while skinny doe-eyed scottish indie boys, old fat goths, freaks, fundamentalists, pouty french actresses and a marvelously quiffed morrissey are parading in front of me; i come violently, but i owe it to morrissey's quiff rather than to my neighbour's tongue- acrobatic as it is, it's never got me through fits of gloom and loneliness; cocks and tongues may fail, but morrissey never disappoints me; i'm pissed though and i need to stack asparagus jars in less than two hours, 690 asparagus jars an hour, it might be more by now, the corporate world changes all the time; my dodgy neighbour is driving me to the supermarket, it's four am, it's cold in his car but i feel excited, like something is about to happen, something other than a dreary shift at the supermarket, something magical, i'm shivering with anticipation, i'm licking and chewing my neighbour's free hand, it tastes nice, everything's looking new and beautiful, the piss-soaked lampposts that i've passed so many times startle me, i'm loving all the neon signs, i'm loving my neighbour, i want him to adopt me, look at those donkeys, i know them, i've caressed them, so sad i have to destroy the people i love, so sad i fail to destroy the people i hate, the supermarket looks plump but strangely endearing, there are seagulls looting the bins, they're producing very upsetting noises, they sound like babies that are being tortured by a kinky nightnurse, or by a malicious grandfather, or by anyone, suffering babies, or rodents for that matter; i kiss my neighbour goodbye and i promise i'll visit him again real soon, the supermarket swallows me, i put on my smudged apron, i sober up, but i'm still tingling with anticipation.

HELP!I'M TRAPPED BETWEEN THE THIGHS OF A KINKY FLEMISH FISHMONGER! / wee andy is leafing through a washing machine manual whilst i skin a grouper, i am wearing black knickers that don't fit my minge, i got them from the retarded flemish cook yesterday, he always buys me black knickers that don't fit my minge, "did you know that groupers never actually copulate?! they just rub themselves against rocks when they're randy, the next grouper who rubs itself against that rock will be impregnated without ever knowing it until her repulsive spawn kicks its way out of her belly", "that's not how fish give birth" wee andy says and continues leafing through his washing machine manual, the grouper is sticky and is- despite having no eyes- looking at me, i throw it in the sink and sit myself in the couch next to wee andy, i put my hand on his crotch, he takes it and presses it against his frail chest, i slap his frail chest and let my hand slide downwards again, "did you know that my father is really famous in south africa?", "famous for what?", "for writing spiteful songs about my minge and for having invented a neonlit device that can simultaneously skin codlings and sing sad french songs", "i see" wee andy says, but i can tell by the smug sarcastic conceited bourgeois tone in his voice that he thinks i'm making it up, i tell wee andy that i dread being a whore tonight, and it's true: i really dread being a whore tonight and laughing at his crap jokes and sucking that pockmarked middle-aged crooked cock, it's going to be dreadful i just know, it was dreadful last night, why would it be any different tonight?! why would the jokes be any better tonight? "a whore to whom?" wee andy asks, "DOES IT MATTER?! TO MY DODGY NEIGHBOUR IF YOU MUST KNOW, YOU FUCKING NOSY INDISCREET CUNT YOU", "tell him your minge has been wolfed down by a shoal of voracious groupers!", "groupers don't swim in shoals, you daft twat", i'm pacing wee andy's living room and thinking about my dodgy neighbour's flabby groin and about all the scary flemish escutcheons that he covers me with after his cum, together they weigh more than a hundred fibre stallions! one weighs almost as much as an obese camel! so you can imagine how bruised and small and stupid i feel after such awkward sex, even if i get paid more for two hours of awkward sex than i get paid for a week of relentless drudgery that consists of neatly stacking jars of seedless californian grapes and counting frozen lobsters and being scolded by venoumous big-nosed corporate cunts, i'm also wondering why my teeth chatter and my buttocks shudder and my cheeks tingle and my armpits ache when he shoves his callous fingers up my arse, i don't have that with other johns, but then other johns don't have such pent-up spite in their wee crooked fingers, and they are usually younger and less flemish, my neighbour is seventy-three, he has a crack addiction and a ghastly russian suitcase full of blue pills, he's extremely far-right wing and extremely into beating up fifty years younger minging french expats, "what are you thinking of?" wee andy asks, but i can tell by the smug nonchalant ironic bourgeois tone in his voice that he doesn't give a fuck, i tell wee andy that i'm thinking of the saggy stark white liver-spotted cock of my dodgy neighbour, "that's disgusting" he says, "i know" i say, "but what's even more disgusting is that i'll be licking it and fondling it and calling it leopold" i look at my stolen tinsel watch, "in less than three hours!!" wee andy doesn't feel sorry for me, he says that compassion is a short term solution and that i should stop cutting my calves with his carving knife, i lay down the knife and stroke the gutted grouper in the sink, i go to wee andy's bathroom, i wash my minge, i bandage my calves, i paint my cheeks, i smoke a fag and watch myself smoke a fag in the mirror, i roll my eyes at the miserable slapper and stub the fag out against my brow.

I ADMIRE YOUR P-R-O-L-I-F-I-C-A-C-Y,BUT I'M NOT A BIG FAN OF YOUR P-U-N-C-T-U-A-T-I-O-N / i feel hopeless to be honest, but not in a smug theatrical way, in an ugly self-indulgent way, mind, my dodgy neighbour says that my hopelessness is very photogenic, he captured it on film last night, he sold the pictures to the kinky nightnurse this morning, the kinky nightnurse called me up an hour ago, he said: "your skinny hopelessness and sunken cheeks won't look so charming six months from now, i suggest you buy a rifle from my albanian friend who lives in that white castle opposite the disused siberian launderette, shoot yourself before you become a bitter spiteful psychotic nuisance", "i'm not psychotic" i said, but he'd already hung up, and now i'm roaming the crooked coastal alleys and arcades, i'm not combing, i'm not looking, i'm not longing, i'm hardly aching for a fuck, ok admittedly i am aching for a flemish crucifix up one of my nether orifices, i don't care whether it's a polish priest or a heathen welsh taxidermist who shoves and pokes it till my eyeballs ooze that brownish pus, i'm not choosy, however, i am very choosy about the jesus nailed to it, if he looks too smug and sanctimonious and unforgiving i don't want him inside me, i fucking hate jesus, he's even more repulsive than buddha, at least buddha didn't force his crippled opinions upon hookers and children, at least buddha didn't con gullible fishermen and desperate winos with all that bloody useless hocus pocus, at least buddha didn't thrust all that guilt upon decent god-fearing orphan girls and lonely mancunian heroin pushers; i sit myself on the bronze feet of a cock-eyed french poet, he looks a bit like the illiterate rentboy: vulnerable and moody, no i haven't read his stuff, but i'm sure it's brilliant and wasted on all these twisted middle-aged locals, a minging russian hobo offers me a fag and a shoulder to cry on and a scabby cock to fondle, i accept the latter, i've quit smoking and sobbing, i unzip his brown curry-stained pants, pull down his tiny black drawers and rub the tip of his cock ferociously but also affectionately, i take it in my mouth and suck it with a cheerful contempt of aids, i swallow his cum and scrounge a fag off him, i bare the most gruesome part of my soul to him, and then i bare my minge, he pokes it with his lighter, and then furtively fingers it, "have you read anything by this boy?", i point at the bronze statue of rimbaud, "no, he's a bit too queer for me", the hobo grabs rimbaud's bronze groin and chuckles obnoxiously, i run away from them, i've been running around barefoot for weeks now, my shoes don't fit anymore, in the bus station next to the cuban brothel and opposite the closed sea life centre someone's spraypainted: "death to the minging self-obsessed barefoot whore with her bloody literary ambitions and her insatiable spite and the grotesque scratches on her groin and all her vulgar confessions, why can't she fucking muster the courage to buy a rifle or a nice reliable rope and shoot or hang herself?" of course it was me who spraypainted that, my enemies aren't that literate, i enter a murky catholic church, there's a young scruffy geezer reading kerouac in a pew, i tear a ghastly etching off the wall and go over to him: "do you know this miserable cunt?" i point at the bearded cunt who's wagging his finger at two gloomy starved peasants, "why of course, that's jesus", "why is he scolding these peasants?", "i don't know", i trash the etching and comb the church for kinky middle-aged clerics, there aren't any, i take a nap in the confessional, a perverted priest rudely shakes me awake, i ruffle my hair and scowl at him: "what do you want? a sordid confession or a ferocious blowjob?" the greedy cunt wants both! i slip under his sacerdotal cloak and drowsily suck his cock, i spit his cum on his sacerdotal brogues and confess to him that i've jerked off a malicious seventy-three year old flemish marksman for two loaves of jewish bread and ten coins last night, but the loaves were stale so i had to wolf down the coins, the priest frowns on me, i clutch his cloak and ask him for forgiveness, "you need to do penance first" he says and shrugs off his sacerdotal cloak, i suck his cock again, less drowsily this time, and i swallow his cum this time, "you're forgiven, now piss off" he snaps, i leave the church, smoke a fag and shrug off all that hopelessness.

BEACH SCUM / fucking coastal decay, i'm not finding it charming at all, fucking disused theatres, sleazy discothèques, obnoxious german tourists, pseudo-rustic cute little houses, treacherous wet sand, vulgar beats coming from pimp vehicles, pervs leering at underage flesh, oddly coloured ice cream, cheap clothes, revolting tans, and that fucking ghastly house where i grew up; and that fucking illiterate rentboy insisted on accompanying me, he's wearing pink sandals and ankle bracelets, he's going through his blatantly queer phase, i liked him better when he was a miserable closet poof; we're here to kill my grandmother, she's a spiteful hag, not to mention an alcoholic and a tart; she's not happy to see us, she's drinking port and she's wearing a golden brooch in the shape of a young girl who's drowning, i pour myself a port, christopher is being his apathetic self, he's watching mtv whilst rubbing his crotch, he's kicked off his pink sandals, my grandmother picks them up, she thinks they're cute, she's flirting with christopher but he's ignoring her, i pour myself another port, the sad old tart is slurring something about some dodgy vet who lives nearby and whom she fancies, she bought a persian cat and poisoned it just to have an excuse to go see him, i put on my walkman, but the volume only goes so loud and occasionally her inadequate patter seeps through: and he broke my radiator, i bought him a bottle of whisky, that clock ticks too loudly, persian cat, cock, cunt, cock, cock, cock, a solid boner for such and old man etc etc, "LIAM,OH MY FUCKING GOD, IT'S LIAM, come on, miserable cunt, you recognise liam, the mancunian sex god, would you look at him, all rough and bearded, let's hump the television set!" but christopher just shrugs and closes his eyes again, "so...anything exciting happening round here, apart from old cunts poisoning their pets for a bit of veterinary love?", "i've joined the AA", "i've joined the socialist union", "i'm trying to cut down on the booze", "i quit smoking", we down another glass of port, christopher is snoring in front of the telly, this is almost idyllic, in a totally fucked up way, i almost love these cunts, in a totally fucked up way; i tell the old hag that i need to use the bathroom, her handbag is lying on her bed, i take all the money, i almost feel guilty when i catch her smiling at me from her passport, pang, and then it's over and i'm looking forward to squandering all this cash with christopher; i can hear french cunts coming from the beach, pow pow pow, there's a magpie staring at me, pow, two stuck-up middle class slags discussing middle class films about working class misery, pow pow; christopher is sitting on my grandmother's lap, she's stroking his hair, i should kill them both, i drag the rentboy off her barren lap and we leave the wretched house and its wretched inhabitant, fucking perverted alcoholic monster beast manipulative tart liar sick kinky cowardly bitch serpent slag; there's an old cunt on the train writing dodgy stories about a minging orphan girl and an illiterate rentboy, every now and then he looks up at us, smirks, and then continues writing, it proper pisses me off, i'm well relieved when the cunt gets off, "wasn't that your father?", "look, a shetland pony!!", "that's not a shetland pony, that's a cow", "whatever", the train is groaning and farting and wheezing, there's no one left on the train but us, christopher's left foot is bleeding, i try to write a story, but the shetland ponies are distracting me.

THE KINKY NIGHTNURSE HAS VINDICTIVE MOLARS AND A FATAL COCK / it's hard to stay sane when doctors fuck you and hiss in your cunt that you're mad, the kinky nightnurse is not strictly a doctor but he's got a white coat and sedatives, that's close enough; ever since i've been trying to avoid him i bump into him all the time, when i'm not with him i doze off and dream about his avenging boner and callous fists, when i wake up i feel like crying, but i can't cry cos it'd upset christopher, he'd start crying as well and when he cries he sounds like a seal in heat, i should know, i went to the zoo yesterday and i stood in front of the performing seals for two hours and they were lecherously belching whilst copulating, it sounded awful, like they were in their death throes, i found it hard to leave them; i bumped into the kinky nightnurse on my way to the cunt that spawned me, it's just as well then that i bumped into him cos i was carrying a knife and had more than half a mind to plant it in her repulsive belly, but the kinky nightnurse snatched it away from me and he's admiring his features in the blade, there's nothing admirable about his perverted features, his nose is crooked and his eyes are so narrow you can never catch him staring at your wounded genitals even though you know he is; we're sitting on a dead tree in the wee forest where i once was fondled by a dutch woman who looked like an orphan boy, i loved her cos she didn't have a cock and she listened to jewish singer/songwriters and she scoffed at all my self-pity, the day after she'd fondled my cunt on the moss and wet leaves she hung herself in her attic, i don't think i'm directly responsible, i went to her funeral and there were lots of dutch women there whom i wanted to fondle, but they were all straight and mourning, i did fuck a priest after the funeral but he had nothing to do with the funeral if that's what you think, he was just a priest whom i happened to bump into in a piss-soaked alley, very malicious he was, he maimed my cunt with a rusty crucifix and scoffed at my tears, i still cried back then when pervs baited my genitals, now i merely shrug cos they'll only hit harder if you cry or cringe, if this coastal town wasn't so goddamn perv-infested i could like it here, but as it is i really hate it, sometimes i can feel the hate gnawing at my heart, it's fear actually; the kinky nightnurse is touching my cunt with his cold fingers, so cold they feel like frozen shrimps, i can hear mammals copulating in nearby shrubs, maybe hedgehogs, maybe eating rather than copulating; i scraped a run over hedgehog off the road yesterday, this was in wee andy's street, many hedgehogs die in wee andy's street, i dropped its remains on wee andy's doorstep, not like a cat would do for its owner mind, i just thought that maybe he could use them remains for one of his art projects, wee andy and all his bloody pretentious art projects, if i wasn't so damn fond of him i could easily hate his guts, or the other way around; the kinky night-nurse's cock is so hard it could bludgeon a hirsute peasant to death, when he enters me i can hear hostile gulls screeching in the distance, but they might be obnoxious toddlers, and they're probably in my head, he cums in my face, his spunk momentarily blinds me, when i can see again i see his balls and cock dangling in front of me, they look kinda pathetic now that they're crumpled up again, but i'm still scared of him, he's stroking my belly with the knife, all the while he's talking feverishly about anorexic orphan boys whom he keeps hostage at the nuthouse, thick gorgeous underage boys with no visitors to give a fuck about the fresh scars and bruises on their cheeks and thighs, many of those thick gorgeous underage boys will become thick spiteful old winos, others will slit their wrists, like darren who was my favourite nutter at the nuthouse cos he wasn't mad at all, not even neurotic, all day we would stand by the wee window in the corridor and watch the world continue without us, it didn't bother us, we were heavily sedated then, until i started hiding the sedatives in my rolled-up pyjama sleeves, from then on it made me cross to think that the world was continuing without me, and when the sedatives were worn out i ran away, darren on the other hand slit his wrists and died, which is always more effective; the kinky nightnurse is biting my thighs, i've never been bitten by a horse but i'm sure it feels like this, after a while the perv gets bored of me, he scratches his groin, punches me in the face and drives back to the nuthouse where he can maim genitals that are much more fragile and much more underage than mine; i run to wee andy's place, i stop in front of his smug white horse, i stretch out my hands and plead with the beast to bite me, but it doesn't budge.

THOM YORKE IS CLEANING THE BEDROOM WINDOWS / "good morning my sweet corporate bastard, you are looking grim today, you look like you've been up all night sitting by your mother's deathbed, mopping up her spittle, piss, mucous and whatnot; well if it wasn't that then you really have no excuse to walk around with a face like that, dammit, i've been sucking retarded flemish cock all night and you don't see me sulking, do you now? sulking is for miserable poofs and illiterate ex-rentboys, not for minging orphan slags, and definitely not for corporate cocks, so how about a smile on that ugly ruddy corporate face of yours? suit yourself, be a miserable poof then, be the laughingstock of the supermarket then, as if i give a fuck, i don't want to work for you anymore, i want to work for someone less corporate and more talkative, in an ideal world i wouldn't be working for any middle class cunt at all of course, in an ideal world i would be working for performing seals, i would feed them fish and pat their smooth lovely heads if they did a really spectacular trick like killing a dolphin whilst jumping through a hoop of fire; ok ok i'll work for you, but i'm not stacking any milk bottles today, only boring people stack milk bottles; i had sex last night, i wouldn't call it amazing, but i did come five times, so i'm not gonna complain, how about you? any sex at all? then why the long face? you had your hole, you should be whistling and making crap jokes; oh before i forget: rudiger called me last night, he misses the supermarket but he doesn't miss you cos he thinks you're a 'rude insensitive racist cunt'- his words- and he hopes you fall off your ladder and break your neck, he's in berlin right now, doing all sorts of tedious german stuff: burning books, beating up hippies and singing hymns, stuff like that, he also went to the zoo and stared down polar bears and crocodiles, of course he might have been lying, you know how germans are: they can't resist giving a twist to the truth; yesterday after work i bumped into the spiteful busker, you know him, don't you? he's the crazy wino who's always singing incest ballads in the car park, anyway, i bumped into him at the library, i was looking for novels about suicidal nocturnal rodents, and i said: 'daddy, what are you doing at the library, i thought you hated books??!!' and he said: 'i'm looking for novels about suicidal nocturnal rodents', and still he insists on denying that he's my father, what a sad tosser, i think he's afraid that i'm gonna ask him for money or tenderness; but i'm not demanding like that, all i want is to go the pub with him and have a conversation about rodents, that's my dream, do you think it's very sentimental?? well sod you, easy for you to be all cynical, you've got money, golden retrievers and non-sleazy relatives, i only have a non-sleazy goldfish and i think it's dead anyway; i want to slit my wrists now, i'm sad now, i want to go home now, i want to shag my dodgy neighbour under the headless cuckoo clock now, i want to swallow rusty nails now, i want to slash my cunt with my bicycle now, i'm sorry, that didn't make sense; let's be friends, let's go to manchester and stack milk bottles there, or better still, let's forget all about the milk bottles and shag each other's brains out, it doesn't have to be in manchester, it can be anywhere; i'm wearing no knickers today cos i've run out of knickers and i dread going to the launderette cos it's full of pervs and fat old ex-whores, they hate me and want to shag me cos i'm young and arrogant, and being shagged by someone who hates you is worse than being snogged by a retarded flemish cook, i'll tell you that much; but you wouldn't know, would you? cos you have a washing machine and i bet you sit in front of it and watch it whirl and feel all smug and superior and scoff at the minging orphan losers who are being harassed at launderettes, pffffff, one day i'll have my own washing machine, that's my dream, do you think it's very middle class?? well sod you, easy for you to be all metaphysical, you've got talking household appliances; no i don't know what 'metaphysical' means exactly, i just wanted to be pedantic; all this talk about washing machines has made me really horny, i mean hungry, i'm really hungry now, so hungry that i feel like ripping open a box of washing powder and snorting it; do you have stuffed seabirds at home? do you talk to them when you get lonely? do you ever get suicidal? have you ever broken someone's nose? have you ever grassed up a friend? of course you have, otherwise you wouldn't be this disgustingly loaded, do you play any instruments? how many times a day do you wank? do you wank at the supermarket? do you think about that nice blond lady who stacks candy bars when you wank at work? i know i do; can i go home now? can i sniff some glue in the bogs before i clock off? don't hate me, adopt me, see you tomorrow, corporate twat!"

THE WORLD'S NOT A DOLPHIN-SAFE PLACE / we're sitting by the artificial waterfall in the park that's named after a dodgy flemish peasant who wrote a few rural poems and arsefucked most of his sheep, not the kind of geezer i'd name a park after; the perv i'm with shares his first name with the dodgy peasant, it's a common enough flemish name that sounds so vile and ominous that i can't even bring myself to pronounce it, so i asked him if i could call him peter cos that's the name of a colleague at work that i fancy and he said yes, he calls me andrea cos that's my name when i sell my genitals to kinky flemish wine merchants, andrea cos my best middle class friend's called andy, although he wasn't the least bit flattered when i told him that i use his name when i suck crippled flemish cock in return for a tenner and tacky china deer with big vulnerable eyes; the wee artificial waterfall reeks of decaying codfish and shit-stained sleeping bags, it's nice to be fucked here, his grunts are smothered by the water and the obnoxious white kids who are playing some ball game nearby, i can even hear the choir rehearse in the bloody catholic church that's opposite the park, the spiteful busker's wailing all over it, which is just as well cos at least his wailing is less ambiguous than theirs, i can hear seedy pub doors creak as endearing winos stagger inside, i can hear vicious cow killers pouring streams of russian abuse on this wretched coastal town and i can't blame them, i hate it as well, it's full of perverted vicars who'll maim your genitals if you tell them you don't believe in god, but it's hard to believe in god if your genitals are constantly baited and if the only ones who believe in god are the ones baiting them; thank god then for this flemish wine merchant who doesn't believe in god but maims my cunt all the same, i asked him if he did cos he wears a little silver cross on his collar, at least that's what i thought, but when i looked closer it turned out to be a ship, and he's an atheist; the grass is still wet from the morning rain and when he arsefucks me i suck the rain from the dead leaves cos i'm terribly thirsty, i've been up all night drinking rum and hating that fucking unfaithful sheffielder cunt, and then i passed out and when i woke up i knew my body needed something, but i couldn't think what it was, so i slashed my arms with the lid of a dolphin safe tuna tin, but i didn't feel any better afterwards, i cycled to the supermarket and when i finally arrived my arms were still bleeding, and since rudiger wasn't there to disinfect and bandage them, they sent me home, but i didn't go home, i roamed the seedy arcades and bumped into this kinky flemish cunt who was up for sex, he was even up for paying for it; my arms are still bleeding, i just hope the perv can't see them or he'll get aroused and ask my genitals to bleed as well, that's why i'm bandaging my arms with dead leaves and a donald duck sweatshirt some obese kid has left behind; we stagger out of the park, actually i'm the only one staggering cos i'm the only one who's just been arsefucked with a thorny branch, and if it wasn't for his old crippled legs he'd be swaggering; we enter the murky coastal pub that's murky cos the church is pouring its accusatory shadow on it, he orders us a cocktail that has the colour of defroster and the name of a whore, i let the old alsatian who's lying in front of the jukebox taste it first, it doesn't drop dead so i down the cocktail and leave the pub, the scruffy alsatian is following me, we sit ourselves by the wee artificial waterfall, there are plastic bags, dead rabbits and broken coat hangers floating in the water, the alsatian is howling at the setting sun, or maybe it's in pain, it's an old crippled alsatian with bald patches on its swollen belly, i call it rooster cos that's its name, it's carved in its red collar, rooster is licking the blood-soaked donald duck sweatshirt that's wrapped around my left arm, i don't think he'll devour me, he's way too domestic for that kind of behaviour, i let him lick my arms, and i let him lick my wounded genitals, i doze off and i dream about gregarious alsatians and about kinky flemish peasants, when i wake up there's a churlish morning sun scoffing at me, my arms are still bleeding and my cunt's being licked by a hirsute flemish geezer.

FAKE SUICIDE,FAKE DOCTOR,REAL GOLDFISH / wee andy is sitting in a corner of his bedroom violently trembling and sobbing, i am standing on his bed covered in blood, i'll admit that it looks impressive, but the wee poof is overreacting, i slit my wrists with my scalpel but i haven't hit any important arteries, i feel fucking alive, this can't possibly be me dying, bleeding to death, no way, i'm jumping up and down on wee andy's bed, after a while i feel dizzy and i want to lie down and close my eyes, christopher keeps slapping me in the face and he wants to make the bleeding stop but i won't let him, it's gorgeous, i feel confident and beautiful, the blood is trickling down my pale puny body, i lift my arms and it trickles into my mouth and onto my face, i can hear sirens but they're far away, no actually they're getting louder, nearer, they're here, i'm bloody well not going back to the nuthouse, i was just having a little fun with my scalpel, but i don't expect these unimaginative over-privileged middle class poofs to understand, and when the first rotten twisted ambulance geezer enters i jump out of wee andy's bedroom window and run away as fast as possible, which is amazingly fast for someone with slit wrists i should add, i tie my arms just above the wrists with the red scarf i originally knitted for the spiteful busker, then kept for morrissey, then promised to my sheffielder angel, and now i've had to cut it in two and i'll never be able to knit such a gorgeous scarf again, which means i'll never be adopted and i'll always spend christmas on my own, which is just as well cos i'd rather be an unsociable cunt than have to spend christmas with a spiteful father who'll mistake me for either a turkey or a lover or both, and he'll be so drunk and maybe he'll be sentimental at first and gently stroke my hair, but his grip will become painful and i'll tell him and he'll punch me in the face with an empty calvados bottle but he'll apologise and maybe it'll be a decent christmas after all, but no, cos then he'll remember what a sad old drunkard he really is and he'll have to take it out on someone and it might as well be this useless slag who's just as arrogant and unfaithful as her despicable mother, and he will shag me and beat me like useless slags get shagged and beaten, and in the morning he will be sorry, and i'll forgive him but i'll feel gutted that i have to wait another year for a decent christmas; at the shopping centre i sit by the fountain and wash the dried-up blood off my face, there are giant goldfish swimming between my legs, i grab one very handsome example and i put it in my backpack, i can hear it clap its fin and my heart breaks, i wonder if the two shallow poofs are looking for me but i bet they're just snogging, shagging and listening to obscure indie albums as if nothing happened, i bet that wee cunt is gyrating like a spazwit as we speak; there's a perv approaching me, he asks if i need help, i say "do i fucking look like i need help from a rotten twisted adult, huh?!" he just sits next to me, pretending to look at the goldfish, when really he's just staring at my tits, or wrists, "i'm a doctor" he finally says, "well that's very comforting to hear, a fucking kinky doctor who'll feel me up in the name of science… ", "those wounds need stitching, i'll drive you to the hospital", we don't speak on the way to the hospital, there's an annoying middle class twat on the radio singing about girls who like boys who treat boys like they're girls who treat boys like they're girls, i turn the rubbish off and i put on my mix tape, it's a long ride to the hospital, i'm waiting for the kinky doctor to put a hand on my thigh or rub my tits but his hands firmly clench the wheel and i can see that he's fighting it and i think he should give in to his innate perversity, and then morrissey is trudging slowly over wet sand, back to the bench where his clothes were stolen, and i tell the sleazy doctor that morrissey's my surrogate father and that he's gonna adopt me, but if you want to adopt me that'd be fine as well, but the doctor merely shakes his head wearily; i am almost relieved when he finally puts a hand on my thigh, unzips my jeans and eventually fingers my insanely throbbing cunt, "you're not a real doctor, are you?" and he just laughs, rather diabolically i should add.

DON'T EAT FISH,CUNT! / one of the backstabbing bitches i stack milk bottles with read my palm under the neon lights last week, she said i was gonna die, a polish lorry that transports plastic christmas trees was supposed to have run me over yesterday morning, but it didn't, it just drove by me and then it was gone; the flemish bitch reread my palm this morning and she said i'm gonna choke on a piece of veal tonight, but i don't eat meat so i'm not too worried; i'm walking home from the supermarket, every time i spot someone coming from the opposite direction i throw myself on the ground and pretend i'm dying, most cunts ignore me, one old lady who's wearing big false teeth and a purple wig strokes my hair and holds me close to her frail chest, i steal her purse, there's nothing but small change in it, i throw it at a cancerous poodle with bulging black eyes and a swollen belly, it's choking on the coins; on the pavement in front of the launderette there's a bearded hobo punching an empty bottle of calvados in his face, it's my father, he pretends not to recognise me, or maybe he really doesn't recognise me, cos when i catch my ghastly reflection in the window of an empty telephone booth i see that my nose is bleeding, there are mud stains and dead leaves covering my cheeks, and i'm wearing a purple wig, i take off the wig and stuff it in wee andy's letter box, he can always use it in one of his plays, miserable closet poof that he is; in the park four obnoxious middle class kids are throwing sticks at a white pigeon, i chase them away, the pigeon is crippled, it's beyond repair, i wrap it in my red scarf anyway, i sit myself on a piss-soaked bench that has a piss-soaked hobo on it and admire the frolicsome ducks and stare down the conceited golden retrievers and their conceited owners; the cripple pigeon is writhing on my lap, i don't think it'll be writhing much longer, it looks so sad and tired, the piss-soaked hobo offers me a cigarette, i take it, it's probably not a hobo if he can offer cigarettes to minging orphan girls, he does reek of piss and swedish tequila, he's telling me about some scottish vixen who works in some glaswegian toy shop and has a ladybird tattooed on the inside of her left thigh and after he kissed it she broke his heart and he asks me do i have a ladybird tattooed on the inside of my left thigh? i haven't, but i have a rash on the inside of my left knee, i don't know if that counts for anything? he asks me if he can stuff the pigeon, cos he's a taxidermist, but the pigeon is not dead, cunt! not dead yet, bitch! the piss-soaked taxidermist offers me a swig from his bottle of spanish gin and a bite from his pineapple jam sandwich, i nearly choke on it; i call my sheffielder angel and tell him that i nearly choked on a pineapple jam sandwich that i got from a piss-soaked taxidermist, he scolds me for accepting pineapple jam sandwich from piss-soaked taxidermists; and cigarettes! and spanish gin i add, he scolds me for accepting cigarettes! and spanish gin! from a piss-soaked taxidermist i hardly know, but i do know him, his heart was broken by a scottish vixen who works in a glaswegian toy shop and has a star tattooed on the inside of her left thigh! i can hear my sheffielder angel chopping vegetables whilst scolding me, i scold him for chopping vegetables whilst scolding me, but they aren't vegetables, they are frozen shrimps, i scold him for eating seafood, i hang up on him; i offer the piss-soaked taxidermist a blowjob, but he just wants my pigeon.

A NEONLIT DEVICE THAT ELECTROCUTES FLIES / christopher and i are sitting in the ghastly cafeteria of the swimming pool, the heating is humming, there's a neonlit box on the ceiling that lures flies inside and then electrocutes them, i'm drinking a green cocktail that's named after a sleazy obese flemish crooner, christopher's drinking stella, we are sitting under the neonlit box and from time to time dead flies drop into our drinks, i fish them out with a spoon and put them on my napkin, maybe i'll bury them in the bleak reservoir next to all those dead hares, we're smoking fags and fantasising about killing that bald junkie who lives in the bedsit above ours, when i bump into him in the corridor he blocks my way with his stolen bike, grabs my left tit and snogs me like he hates my guts, he lost all his hair the night he got raped by two geezers, one of them was his father, he was being fellated by his father and his long brown locks just died off and fell on his father's nape and back and after they were done with him he had not a single hair left on his bruised body, that's what christopher told me, that's what he told christopher, there's a lash on christopher's cheek, i pluck it from his face and tell him that he should close his eyes, throw it behind his back and make a wish, he says that i can have his wish, i don't know if the wish counts when the eyelash isn't yours, but i close my eyes, throw christopher's lash over my shoulder and make one anyway, i'm wishing tuberculosis on that bald junkie, christopher says that we could steal his heroin supply and put icing sugar in its place, or we could put an innocent-looking basket filled with poisoned bread and arsenic-soaked kippers on his doorstep cos he always scrounges bread and kippers off us, or more effective still: we could shove a wooden spike up his arse and set it on fire, we snigger when we imagine him rocketing off, colliding with the sinister belfry and smacking against the cold cobbles; christopher is still wearing his red trunks, he wants to take a dive from the highest diving platform when he's mustered enough courage and is drunk enough to dive from any height into any pool or hole, we buy new drinks and listen to the massacre above our heads, they crackle when they fly against the purple neonlit pole, both our napkins are full of dead flies, christopher downs two shots of flemish gin and heads for the pool, he's looking all stern and solemn, he's also badly staggering, don't forget to take a picture he says, from the window i watch the silly rentboy climb all the steps, slipping cos they're wet and he's drunk, he's trembling on the highest diving platform, clutching the balustrade, he finally jumps off the board and dives quite clumsily, he lands on his belly, ouch; i buy another cocktail and light another jamaican cigar, christopher enters the cafeteria, he's looking all smug and righteous, like he's just fought in a war, "did you take a picture?" he asks, "of course i did" i say, when christopher's at the bar ordering a well-deserved shot of rum, i take a picture of a boy who's trembling on the highest diving platform and looks nothing like christopher; we down our drinks and stagger out of the cafeteria and into a churlish autumnal afternoon, we watch shopwindows of music stores and try to imagine what the sleeves sound like, a flemish perv is coming towards us, it's the retarded flemish cook, he buys us all the albums we've been looking at, he even buys us albums we haven't been looking at, we're walking back to our dreary bedsit, i dread getting snogged in that sinister corridor; we enter the tenement, the bald junkie pushes me against the wall, grabs my left shoulder and slides his tongue inside my mouth, i hold my tongue still and try to shrug off his hands, after ten minutes he finally puts his tongue away and swaggers out of the tenement, i bite my fist, rip off an eyelash, close my eyes, throw it over my left shoulder and wish my sheffielder angel would adopt me and teach me how to sell spreadsheets and tuck me in every night and fuck me hard but not wake me up to fuck me hard if i was sleeping; we sit ourselves in my shower tray and listen to songs we already know, i put the batch of albums the retarded flemish cook bought us in our cupboard, the retard says that we owe him so much by now we could never live long enough to pay him back, but that doesn't mean we shouldn't try, so we try to pay him back, all afternoon we pamper his retarded genitals, he's hardly grateful, he leaves at six pm, christopher and i walk back to the swimming pool cos we forgot the dead flies and we both need to dive off the highest platform.

ME AND MY WEE WASHING MACHINE / what do you mean there's a strike?? you can't do this to me, i need to stack milk bottles, it cleanses my soul, fucking communist cunts, fucking union scum, i hate you!! no supermarket then, well that's just fucking wrong, i feel like an orphan again, a mean minging self-destructive scruffy orphan girl, this is an ugly start of another dreary day, and the sun hasn't even come up yet, the limping cats and morning birds are terribly vibrant though, i don't really want to slaughter them, but i do fantasise about squeezing the life out of those soft feathery chests and fluffy emaciated bodies; of course that sheffielder cunt won't pick up his phone, but i have to talk to him, i want to tell him that a giant kangaroo is gonna adopt me and i'm gonna live in her pouch and there'll be room for my rentboy sidekick, my scissors and my smiths cds, but there won't be any room for him, and i also want to tell him that i read his bloody awful poetry and it's mediocre, and i'm not gonna cry myself to sleep cos the cunt doesn't want to read my stories any more, i'm going over to sheffield sex city and i'm gonna plaster it with my stories, and i'm also gonna have to plaster leeds, cos that's where he works;

i'm in my bedsit and i'm wearing my smudged apron and stacking cheese and condoms, but it's just not the same, and the insensitive rentboy is laughing at me, this is what he says: "you're soooooooooooooooooo pathetic", and when he says "sooooooooooooooooooo" his head wiggles like he's some illiterate whoring retard, which incidentally he is; "let's go to the launderette, christopher, maybe there'll be people there who are thicker, nastier and uglier than us, and even less eloquent than you, and even more pathetic than me!!" we're heading for the launderette, christopher is wearing a leather bracelet with the name "gavin" carved in it, what a sick fuck, gavin is his nefarious pimp, the rentboy wants to be less romantic about hustling scum, yeah yeah i know, the pot calling the kettle romantic, but at least i'm not wearing a bracelet that says "the cunt that spawned me", or "the spiteful busker", or "dodgy neighbour", or whatever cunt's trying to destroy me these days; christopher and me- christopher and i?? i suck at grammar, that's how i met my sheffielder angel, he was my special teacher at that special charity school where they dumped me cos no one else would have me; he was supposed to cure me of my invented dyslexia and teach me some basic grammar skills, he bloody well failed, didn't he??! anyway, christopher and i are walking hand in hand and singing oasis songs, the sun is shining, there are little blue flowers growing between the cracks in the pavement, tis all pretty idyllic until the spiteful busker spots us and here he comes now, foaming and trembling with anger, his nostrils are two huge holes that are trying to suck us up, christopher isn't scared, he knows my father's probably not gonna kill him, and besides he's too thick to be scared of death, "what do you have to say for yourself?" erm, what's the cunt on about?? "ignore me, i'm drunk", "cool, bye then", but he's following us, i'm not liking this, he might stab me in the back, that'd be just his style, i'm walking backwards so that i'm facing him, if he's so keen on killing me, he might as well look me in the eyes, he owes me that much; after having fallen in a few concrete mixers and puddles and lakes and gutters, i finally arrive at the launderette; my father and christopher are discussing tintin, TINTIN FOR FUCK'S SAKE, isn't he fictional? isn't he boring? isn't he belgian? TINTIN LOATHES RENTBOYS AND INCESTUOUS SWINE, YOUSE CUNTS WANT TO LOOK FOR A NEW ROLE MODEL, and that has shut them up; there's an old alcoholic hag ironing her tablecloths, there are two poofs watching their poof clothes tumble dry as if it's the most exciting show they've seen all week, it probably is; there's a stuck-up middle class slag reading catch 22 and pretending not to hear my father sing his spiteful incest ballads- yes, they can be spiteful and still be ballads, the oxford dictionary is on my side; i put my smudged apron and spunk-stained knickers in washing machine number three, it's a wee washing machine, its steel-coloured frame is rusty and chipped and someone's written "i fucked three black women on this machine" on the washing powder lid or whatever it's called; my father's leaving, he needs his sad old man's kicks and calvados, christopher is chatting up some miserable monobrow closet poof who's wearing a purple scarf, there's a star tattooed on his left earlobe, fucking unfaithful rentboy- yeah yeah, pleonasm, i know; there's a fat old ex-whore dumping all her sorry tales on me and showing me her scars from when she was stabbed by her johns and sons and pimps etc etc, i tell her about my wretched life, only to get rid of her, my life isn't really wretched, tis a bit unlucky and dangerous at times, but only a self-indulgent cunt would moan about that, not me, oh no; i'm writing odes to christopher's throbbing genitals on all the washing machines, christopher's embarrassed when really he should be flattered, it's not as if i write about anyone's throbbing genitals, it's not as if i write about my sheffielder angel's throbbing genitals, it's not as if my sheffielder angel is genderless, he's wee though in that department, so wee and so fucking sensitive.

SOPPY POEMS BY A PSYCHOPATH / we're meeting in the dunes, i'm getting ready at my grandparents' house, my grandmother is drunk as usual and she's pissed her pants and still the old repulsive hag thinks i'm gonna listen to her rants about dodgy french philosophers, fuck that for a laugh, you useless old drunkard, i pour myself another whisky and i think about black dogs and grandfathers with rifles cos there's nothing else to think about really, all the while the old stinking vicious cunt is slurring big theories and i've no idea what the fuck she's on about, all i know is that they all involve guilt, she doesn't seem too bothered by feelings of guilt, or else she's doing a great job hiding it, and i want to ask her if she feels guilty about having indulged her ex-husband's perversities, but i can't get the words out, i'm sure the answer would be a disappointment, i don't want an answer anymore, i don't want an apology cos i've threatened the bitch so many times that any apology would be fear-induced, not guilt, so fuck her and fuck me too; i'm getting arsefucked in the dunes by two french geezers in about an hour, i hope they beat me up so i can go and lie on wee andy's doorstep bleeding trembling wounded terrified, he'll take care of me, disinfect my wounds ever so fatherly and i'll pretend i'm in shock, the wee gullible cunt still falls for that, as if any amount of violence could shock me now; guns, knives, crowbars, baseball bats, toggled hand harpoons... you name it, it's been shoved up my arse, in all my orifices, i've been left for death so many times, pffff; i just want to be comforted by the wee doe-eyed middle class cunt cos i fancy him, that's all there is to it, and i don't even know what his cock looks like, i've had all the cock i've met, wee andy's just a fucking prude, i bloody well stripped so many times in front of the wee ungrateful twat, i shoved my slashed cunt into his face and he wasn't even aroused, is the cunt frigid or what?! i'm bloody well gonna rape him if he carries on like this, i bet the poof is still a virgin, and who is he saving it for anyway? some stuck-up middle class bitch? i'll bet they'll have post-coital chats about insipid yankee novels and obscure russian art movements, i bet those post-coital chats will last longer than the actual shag, i bet she doesn't even know how to properly suck his cock; i laugh when i think about how uneventful their days will be, and how bored with each other they'll grow, and then they'll die, fat and cynical, i'll be long gone by then, i'm not staying around to watch this generation of complacent self-righteous yuppie scum grow fat, bored, bitter and spiteful, such a sad show, and i wasn't made to be a spectator, my vision is all warped anyway, or that's what they tell me, but i think i'm pretty lucid, far more lucid than these complacent bourgeois cunts at any rate, so don't fucking tell me i'm not in the right frame of mind, i know exactly where i come from, i know that people everywhere are inherently evil, everyone but wee andy and my sheffielder angel, all the other rotten twisted adults are just out to destroy me and some of them even expect me to be grateful, like hell i am, but i'm digressing; my grandmother has put a big wooden box on the table, it contains my grandfather's bloody sentimental poems, if someone who didn't know him would read them they'd think these are bloody touching poems, i wish i'd had a grandfather like that; and they are touching, and therefore they are fake, and therefore i throw them into the fire, i'll fucking expose the cunt as the brutal rapist he was, not some soppy sentimental poet, a fucking merciless psychopath who videotaped his grandchildren tied gagged raped by all his dodgy acquaintances, who shot my black dog, who broke my nose with a shovel, who hugged me so tightly that he broke my ribs, who threw me out the window, who locked me in the basement, who stole my stories and smiths tapes, none of his poems are about rape or any violence at all, they are so inoffensive, so bloody innocuous, they almost make me doubt my own memory, and if it wasn't for all the scars i'd probably end up thinking i was the rotten twisted one, but i'm not, he is, and these fucking sentimental poems are merely ashes now; my grandmother's crying, the tears of a drunkard, i don't feel sorry for the cunt, and it's not like i just destroyed a heart-staggering work of genius either, pull yourself together fucking appalling drunkard, you married the wrong guy, you lived the wrong life, you spawned the wrong children, you said the wrong things, you read the wrong books and you wore the wrong clothes, it's too late to undo all your faults, now get over it and die; i slam the door behind me, i walk to the dunes, a little anxious for all my war talk and my supposed fearlessness, i'm nothing but a defenseless orphan girl that can so easily be slaughtered without anyone even noticing, fuck this for a laugh, i'm not defenseless, the two french geezers are standing by their car at the entrance of the dunes, we walk into the dunes, right to the spot where the dunes merge into the woods, quite a wonderful place, quite a wonderful place for a few hours of relentless hidings and ugly north french abuse.

SHUT UP SKUNKPUSSY! / taking up self-harm again has been the greatest decision i've made, i love to watch the blood dripping on the oasis posters i spread all across the floor of my sorry bedsit, i'm pretty sure liam wouldn't see the warped beauty of this perfectly orchestrated self-destruction, but then i don't even see it myself and i know it will make for a depressing sight in the morning, i will be sober in the morning, i constantly feel bloated, like the spunk is gathering inside me, somehow deforming me, turning me into this slatternly slag, white trash, wasting my days listening to depeche mode, getting boozed up, chatted up, shagged by some pedantic yuppie who only shags me cos he thinks that poor is cool, and where is wee andy when i need him? my skull is itching, i'm scratching my skin until it bleeds and when it bleeds i put a knife to it cos it's never enough, it can never stop; i've written your name on my wall with a black marker: peter, peter, peter, peter, peter, peter, peter, peter, peter, peter, peter peter jolly wife beater... in all sizes, in all styles: plain capitals, girly, curly, childish, non-jointed, closely entwined, imitating as truthfully as possible your handwriting, my father's, my neighbour's, wee andy's, my sheffielder angel's, they're all there, peter, calling you, i am calling you: "come back peter, all is forgiven, and if you want to kill me, then i'm fine with that, just come", i am calling him now and i can tell that he's getting very annoyed with me... oh so i'm an obsessive stalker now, is that it?! well fuck you, miserable moody junkie scum, i hope you OD, bloody unfaithful fag, i'll just stalk someone else then... browsing my precious directory... the sleazy nurse? no, too long ago, my neighbour? no, too close, noel gallagher? if only... i'll have to settle for my father, "you're losing the plot", that's what my neighbour always says to me when i go to him, i don't know what he means, but i have a fair idea: it means fuckall, it means he wants to make me out to be some lost little girl, it means he wants the minge, he's getting the minge, he's getting a whole lot more, i've never went down on him this ferociously, i need the cock so badly tonight; i need the spunk in my hair, the balls in my face, i need the pubic hair and the saggy flesh, i need for him to arsefuck me on the couch, i need to be slapped, gagged, bitten, poked, i need his boner, i need the cum, i need it now, relentlessly, ugly, violently, loveless.

A DEAD DOG AND A ROTTEN TWISTED TAXIDERMIST / there's a dead dog lying in the piss-soaked corridor, it's ian, well that's what i called him, after ian curtis, they both had those big sad eyes screaming injustice and loneliness and bottled up anger, ian was a stray dog, he just entered this wretched housing scheme one day and he never left cos that's what happens to all creatures who enter this godforsaken building, they are locked stuck depressed and addicted, be it budgies, goldfish, junkies, orphan boys, oasis obsessed slags or stray dogs, once you're in you don't get out, and nobody around here dies a natural death- suicide, OD or murder; do dogs commit suicide? i don't know, all i can see is that ian's got terrible stab wounds in his chest, oh to think that beautiful shiny black chest will never heave again, poor ian, i can't stop crying, i promise i will punish whoever did this to you, i will shove a frozen lobster up his arse, cut off his cock with a rusty fork, break his nose with a crowbar and i will stuff a dog collar down his throat and i'll sit on his face to smother his last sorry cries and pleas and i will gloat as i will feel his puny body struggle and gradually lose resistance, oh ian, your beautiful beady eyes, they still blaze so ferociously, maybe i can reanimate you? but it's useless, ian's dead, he hasn't gone down without a struggle, i can tell by the scratches on the floor, brave ian, i will take care of you now, i wrap ian in my black sweater from sheffield sex city and i hope it somehow makes up for that horrendous execution, why kill a dog? why kill ian? it's not like he's carrying money around with him, he hasn't even got a dog collar, or golden teeth, or whatever, pfffff, i take ian outside, it's still dark, it's about four am, i'm carrying a dead dog in my arms, i'm stark naked, i have no idea where i'm going, if only wee andy could see me now, he'd understand my distress, i told him about ian, i told him i loved ian more than him, he wasn't offended, he kinda understood or maybe he was afraid to disagree cos i think i was pointing a gun to his head when we had that conversation, oh well, i don't wanna bury ian, heaven forbid he would end up next to the bones of my rotten twisted grandfather, heaven forbid his bones would arsefuck and batter ian, it's an unbearable thought, i'll take him to a taxidermist, now there's a great idea, i'll have him stuffed, he can keep my stuffed seagull company when i'm out stacking milk bottles and sucking dodgy cock, i'll have to ask the taxidermist to do something about the fear in his eyes though, otherwise i'll never sleep again, i don't mean it like oh let's give him a foolish cheerful grin and stupidly happy eyes like he just died a peaceful death at the feet of his old friendly owner, no, but can we just pretend he wasn't brutally slaughtered by some vicious sex drugs food love compassion money deprived junkie? and can we please wipe the blood, spunk and shit off his chest? and could you give him back a left ear? it seems to have been bitten off, and he also used to have a cock and a tail, and they used to wag when he saw me enter the building and mount the blood-drenched syringe-littered stairs, oh but where do i find a taxidermist? and i don't have any money, i'll just have to get my tender homosexy wee andy to lend me some dough, although i think he's still mad at me after i so brutally tied him and sort of assaulted him and shagged his donkeys and made him watch me wank with scissors, but even an insensitive self-obsessed poof like him will have to understand the importance of getting ian stuffed; i'm carrying my sweet ian in my arms and he's really heavy, like i'm carrying ian and death itself, i'm sweating, hobos on piss-soaked benches are giving me odd looks, dirty looks, like i'm some kind of killer, but i didn't kill ian, you thick useless illiterate drunkards, you want to be a little nicer to me if you don't wanna end up with a dagger in your groin, but they just laugh at me, so coldly and angrily, i run away terrified and crestfallen, those hobos used to be my friends, i used to recite my daft poems to them, my liam gallagher impersonation cracked them up, but now they're just as cruel as everyone else i know bar morrissey and christopher, i finally arrive at wee andy's place, when the donkeys notice me, they run away mournfully braying, but i never meant to hurt them, you're a bunch of over-sensitive ungrateful cunts and you should be drowned, that's what i tell them but of course i don't mean it, i'm just offended by their harsh rejection, i hope wee andy doesn't react to my appearance like his fat ugly stupid donkeys, but of course he does, the cunt opens the door but when he sees it's me, he wants to slam the door in my face, too late silly poof, i'm already inside, this is ian, ian's dead, he's been slaughtered by some junkie, i found him in the corridor two hours ago, he's still warm, touch him andy, by the way why are you wearing a jockstrap? how's your pervy uncle from dorset? when are you gonna visit him? can i come with you? can i kill him for you? i would, you know, i'm not a big fan of rotten twisted adults who feel up tender homosexy indie kids... now how about some money for that taxidermist? i'll give it back as soon as the retarded flemish cook returns from thailand, i'm willing to suck his cock for hours on end, oh he can even rant about pastry while i'm at it, i don't care, it's for a good cause... what's wrong with yer donkeys? they seem a bit traumatised... do you know a good taxidermist in the neighbourhood? your uncle's a taxidermist??! and so it happens that i'm in dorset carrying a dead dog in my arms wrapped in a black sweater from sheffield sex city, a beautiful anorexic homosexy indie boy silently walking next to me... you know, wee andy, after your uncle's stuffed ian, i might just kill him and stuff him as well, i'll give his face an eternal rotten twisted look and he would be holding his cock in his hands like he's about to wank over you, great plan or what?

two

FAMILIAR,BUT NOT LIKE A SONG / i am roaming bleak coastal streets that i've often roamed before, i woke up this morning paranoid and cross and restless and hungover, i thought to myself: "another fucking dreary day with nothing but jerking off four kinky flemish fishmongers to look forward to, and maybe if i get lucky i'll get to suck my sheffielder angel's conceited cock, pfff, you know what? sod them, i'm gonna roam bleak coastal streets that i've never roamed before, maybe if i get lucky i'll get to jerk off kinky flemish fishmongers whom i've never jerked off before!" i got sluttily dressed, i took my bag, stuffed my stanley knife, my lithium, my rope, my walkman and my smiths tape into the bag, strapped it to my throbbing back and left my drab bedsit, i've been roaming for six hours, i couldn't find any coastal streets that i hadn't roamed before and i didn't have enough money for the train, so i just roamed the familiar ones, exciting things have happened, but i'm not gonna tell you about them cos you might go to the police and tell them that it was the minging orphan girl who burned down that seedy coastal pub opposite the sinister south african supermarket, i burned it down cos i was hungover, and also: the owner is a malicious middle-aged german dwarf who once tried to bludgeon me to death with an anvil and who once tried to drown me in a bucket of lentils, and who once poured petrol on my groin and set it on fire, and who once took shots of my bleeding thighs and minge and stuck them to the window of his pub, and who once shoved a coyote skull up my arse, and who always pours me really stingy shots of rum, it's bloody hard to go straight when you roam perv-infested coastal streets and when you're out of your head on austrian crack and cheap red wine, here's another perv now, i try to dodge him, but alas, we collide, he's got a big crooked nose and slender fingers, i start moaning to him about my sheffielder angel's inefficient fingering technique and about his limited empathy and about his tiny hostile genitals and about his shopping sprees which he allows me to watch but not to participate in, i'm only moaning to chase this perv away, but he just pats my chest, and then he yanks my arm and drags me into an all too familiar lugubrious reservoir, "whatever you do, don't call me emma when you rape me, i really fucking hate that name", "i make the rules, not you, EMMA", the sun is setting, the hares are drowsy and slow, he's got thin eyebrows and a weak chin, last week the illiterate rentboy and i buried a canadian chipmunk somewhere in this reservoir, next to the meandering roots of a majestic shrub, it didn't die of old age, far from it, it was young and frisky when a perverted cuban priest shoved it up christopher's arse, it burrowed frantically and suffocated, the priest said that it was the rentboy's fault, typical, the rentboy believed him, the flemish perv tears the bag off my traumatised back and flings it at a gloomy donkey who's biting its blood-stained flank, he pushes me down onto the sand and rips off my jeans and black knickers, he sniffs at them and then stuffs them in his pocket, "do you want to know what my favourite oasis song is?", "no, emma, i don't want to know what your favourite oasis song is", "my favourite tom waits album?" he punches me in the stomach and then starts to finger me, he frowns when he fingers me, he rolls me onto my belly, licks my back, bites my buttocks, spits on my shins, "columbia", "what??", "columbia is my favourite oasis song", "i told you i wasn't interested, bitch", he kicks me in the lungs and punches me in the back of my head till i'm seeing gorgeous golden spots that aren't stars nor satellites, the flemish perv kicks me one last time and then walks away, "FOREIGN AFFAIRS IS MY FAVOURITE TOM WAITS ALBUM" i shout at the retreating flemish perv, it's too dark to dig up the chipmunk, i close my eyes and watch the golden spots land and then take off again, i open my eyes and put my clothes on, at least he left me some money, tomorrow i'll take that train and roam bleak coastal streets that i've never roamed before.

A FEW STITCHES,BUT NO STRINGS / i think i'm gonna give in to my craziness, i'm just gonna fucking indulge myself in the inappropriate speech and the slander and the spite and the self harm and the stalking, funny how everything that makes life sweet and spicy begins with an "s", except for sobriety, that also begins with an "s" but that's not my scene, shrove tuesday is more my kind of show, mind, i skip the lent, i'll stuff my face with sizzling sugary sherry-soaked squid slices if i want, whenever i want, but to be honest i'm not too keen on squid, but that's not the point, the point is that i want to spoil all my senses and shoot myself before they start to stink and spit and sweat and fester, even though the latter begins with an "f", all these sultry sentences have made me bloody randy, i'm dying for a wholesome solid spanking, by the way i am smoking fags- i was tempted to say "spliff" but it'd be a lie, and lying's a sin, and i'm still practicing on my sainthood, though it may not look that way- on the piss-soaked doorstep of a closed pharmacy; i could do with some lithium, it's very nice to be bipolar if i'm on the right pole, but the pool i'm in right now is a bit too noisy and violent, i get up and start running, but then i realise that i'm stuck with myself and with all these prissy french bitches in my head, not to mention the self-deprecating cockney sluts, i hide inside a telephone booth and call wee andy, he's sane and sensible enough for the both of us: "hello?", "andy, it's me, your supposedly insane best friend", "delphie, what can i do for you?", "one: you could stop calling me delphie, call me polly instead, two: you could lend me a few wads and not expect to get them back, three: you could read my latest story and call it bloody marvelous, four: you could let me rip off your clothes and give you the most ferocious blowjob you'll ever receive", "you know i can't let you do the latter, POLLY, but all those other things i'm willing to do, how much money do you need?", "you are too fucking sweet", i hang up on that wee over-privileged saint, why can't he be stingy? why does he have to be so nice? it breaks my heart, it makes me really angry, it's so fucking easy to be straight and generous, there's nothing brave about giving people what they want, fucking smug wee coward, i love him so much, i wish he'd spurn me, then i could finally completely revel in my self-destruction, stop rambling phony nutter! i run out of the telephone booth and into the library, i sit myself in the reading room: "hale knew", i fling the book at a demented toothless twisted local, i can't concentrate, i leave the library, i take the bus to wee andy's, i sit myself in the back, squint and drivel like a retarded whore, then i start squealing wonderwall, i can hear the other passengers gently humming: "ignore the nutter in the back, she's not our responsibility", i get off at the disused armenian jockstrap factory and run to wee andy's house, i knock on his door anxiously frantically: "polly, it's good to see you, i was a wee bit worried when...", "please don't call me polly, call me liam instead", i walk into his kitchen and pace it, "what's wrong, liam?", i snigger, it's nice being called liam, i swagger and spit on the floor, "i am so scared, andy", "why are you scared?", "i stabbed my sheffielder angel last night, i stabbed him in the shins with my stanley knife, and now he's got stitches and an obese mancunian lawyer who says that i'll go to prison if i ever come near him again, i'm terrified of going to prison, but i'm also terrified of a life without those endearing black testicles", i sigh and pour myself a glass of liverpudlian cider, wee andy is stroking my hair and gently lamely scolding me, i take a swig from the glass and shudder, it's too fucking strong, it's poison, i smash the glass in the sink and slash my left arm, "delphine!!", "LIAM!!" wee andy squeezes my hand until i drop the broken glass, he disinfects and bandages the gash, "why can't you be this nice to my other gash?", "shut up, delph", i shut up and bask in the soothing murmur of wee andy's household appliances.

CARE TO CORRUPT ME?FANCY A SHAG? / so much time on my hands, it's awful, and all my hobbies are so perilous and illegal, i can only carry them out in the dark, but it's summer and it never gets dark, or when it finally does get dark i'm too pissed to ride wild horses and jump off wild horses into barbed wire where i'm stuck and bleeding to death whilst being arsefucked by gangs of vicious russian cow killers; thank god for christopher's bulging crotch then, i can lose afternoons staring at it, and i badly need to get rid of my afternoons, these murderous summer afternoons are the worst, it's like every sunbeam is coaxing me into killing myself; i shuttered the windows but now the rentboy's moaning about being claustrophobic, pffff, like hell he is, he spent most of his life locked in basements and cupboards, besides he can always walk out, i am walking out, i'm fed up with his manipulative attention-seeking rentboy ways; i'm not going very far, i'm gonna pay my dodgy neighbour a dodgy visit; there's a few half-witted half-dead junkies littered across the piss-soaked corridor, i tell them where i'm going, just in case, not that they'll remember it when they're high on rat poison, glue, defroster, underage orphan boys and whatnot; my dodgy neighbour is delighted to see me, and so he should be, not every seventy-three year old repulsive ex-wine merchant has an eager orphan girl next door, and definitely not one who's so keen on scissors and rodents; he's telling me about his "art project", i'm not interested, "i'm not interested", he's telling me anyway, it's a series of nude paintings of his grandson, "it's a perv project then", he's not amused, he's explaining to me how it's art rather than a 73-year old perv wanting to wank over his ten year old grandson, his explanation sucks, he's a perv, not an artist; yes, some people can be both, but he is not one of those people; since we're talking about perversities dressed up as art, i tell him about my stories, but i can tell that he's not interested, i can tell cos he just left the room; he's back now, with a bottle of geneva; i down three glasses, but i still feel fidgety and angry; the cunt has proper pissed me off with his supposed art project, not to mention his blatant indifference towards my supposed art project; i down another glass, but instead of covering up the squalor, this dose of booze pushes my face right into it: so much ugliness, most of it tangible, most of it sitting next to me wheezing and staring, i get up and run down the stairs, the door's locked, i should have known, more geneva it is then; the sleazy cunt has put on some fuckawful flemish schlagers which he deems "romantic", but there's nothing romantic about a minging orphan girl who's so fucking bored that she wastes her afternoons shagging a kinky old racist pig whom she loathes, and when she realises just how much she despises him, she tries to run away, but it turns out that he's locked all windows and doors, and then he puts on fuckawful flemish ballads to coax her into sucking his cock, or actually it's the kitchen knife that does the coaxing; none of this is very romantic in my book, it's not that i'm a prude, it's that i expect older people to be caring rather than corrupting, not that i ever actually met a caring older person in real life, but i do occasionally come across them in movies and novels; this specimen definitely isn't the caring kind, it's not like i didn't already know, it's that he always comes up with new t(h)reats, new rodents, new daggers, new scissors, new angles, more violence, more blood, more salt, more wire, more money, longer hours, longer suffering, longer recovering, less time between dodgy visits.

GOD HATES MINGING ORPHAN GIRLS / i enter the church looking for pervs but there's nobody here, not even dour cunts on the wall cos it's a protestant church, nothing here but an empty cross and an altar without an altar cloth; i call wee andy and i ask him to come and pick me up cos i'm too scared to walk home alone, of course he doesn't believe that i'm in a ghastly protestant church in a french coastal town, for if i'm in a church what's with all the racket? those are angels singing, daft twat, i brought my portable stereo with me, isn't a minging orphan girl allowed to play a few oasis songs in a ghastly protestant church in a french coastal town? or is that blasphemous as well? and if i told you i was wanking with a stanley knife in a pew, and that i just carved the sermon on the mount in my belly, and that i shat on the altar and pissed in the holy water font and spraypainted vulgar poems on the church walls and shouted abuse at that cunt above and... the line goes dead, well that's just great, i'm trapped then, in a fucking protestant church somewhere between belgium and france; i am wanking with a stanley knife in a pew when this old cunt enters the church and sits himself next to me, he's not that old actually, he's wearing a golden necklace and he's very tanned, i decide to hate him; he tells me that he's got a house and it's snug and not so far and i can listen to music there and eat something and have something to drink and if i want to i can suck his cock there as well but he's not gonna force me to, that's not the kind of man he is, although he knows for a fact that any other man would take advantage and would force me to suck their cock; we walk to his snug house and he wants to carry my portable stereo and my suitcase but i won't let him cos i don't want his filthy fingerprints all over my not-so-precious belongings, there are scruffy beasts roaming the streets, actually they are old people but they are all hunched and they move like crazy wounded orphan beasts, they bare their false teeth as i pass them by, i put on my stereo and they're all old and scared and laughable; his house is far and not snug at all, but it's too late now to go back; he puts off the music when we're inside, he gives me something sweet and alcoholic to drink and starts moaning about his rough fisherman's life, all the other younger bastarding fishermen are ruining the trade with all their bastarding money and engines and tourists and getting pissed whilst on sea and shagging sirens and whatnot; i tell him about my rough milk bottle stacker's life and all the other older bastarding milk bottle stackers who are ruining the trade with all their gossip and backstabbing and strikes and being dour and sensible whilst on the job and not shagging the minging orphan girl and refusing to cause supermarket mayhem with her and whatnot; i snog him before he can start moaning again, his tongue tastes of beer and buttermilk; he throws me on the ground and rips off my clothes, his hands are trembling and i want to help him unlace my shoes but he pushes me back onto the wooden floor, it's dusty and my nose is running, i ask him if i can blow my nose, but he's not listening, he's licking the back of my thighs, and the inside of my thighs, and then the inside of my cunt, just as i'm about to come church bells start to chime and that's always a huge turn-off; the fisherman does his best to reanimate my cunt, but it's over, i'm cold and sad, i tell him that i want to go back to my bastarding milk bottle stacker's life, not before you suck my cock will you go back to your bastarding milk bottle stacker's life he tells me; i suck his cock and it tastes of salt and wheaten bread, i suck it until it spurts, i let him cum in my face; i am treading through a bleak marshy meadow, i fall a couple of times, there are brown big-headed horses laughing at me, i get rid of my suitcase and call wee andy, i tell him that i'm treading through a bleak marshy meadow and i've fallen a couple of times, there are big awkward beasts laughing at me and i fear that they may well devour me, i am somewhere between france and belgium, there's dried-up spunk caked around the corners of my mouth, the locals want to kill me, the tanned fisherman is not to be trusted, please come and pick me up.

A LUMP OF ANXIETY AND A MISERABLE PONY / i'm talking to a sweet gullible doctor, i was on my way to wee andy, i wanted to borrow an insipid yankee novel from him to pass those dreary tuesday afternoons when no one wants to fuck me, but then i spotted the bespectacled doctor smoking fags in front of a bronze flemish poet, i went over to him, touched his sleeve and started moaning about all the pets that my grandfather shot, and about all my graham greene novels the illiterate rentboy pawned, and about all my dreadful poems wee andy plagiarised, and about all the blowjobs my dodgy neighbour didn't pay enough for, and about all my oasis b-sides that i gave to my sheffielder angel in a mad fit of generosity, and i've been raving for two hours now and he still hasn't touched my minge, he's rubbing my left shoulder all ambiguously fatherly, some of the stuff i tell him is true, most of the stories i tell him are the ones christopher tells me on monday when we catch our breath and exchange gruesome tales, tales about the flemish pervs we've jerked off and sucked too ferociously, his stories are always more exciting than mine cos he gets fucked by priests and taxidermists and i mostly by dour german businessmen; the sweet gullible doctor and i sit ourselves on the rain-soaked doorstep of a closed book store, we're sitting on his thick russian paper but can still feel the rain, he's not russian, the paper's for his waiting room, he's got quite a few russian patients, when i get bored of talking to him i snatch the paper from under his bottom and try to read it, i cut out an article about fox hunting and a picture of liam gallagher and give him back the paper, we smoke some fags and watch each other's eyeballs, i try to look solemn and noble and tragic all at the same time, but i get shy and bury my head under his smug winter coat, it's nice and safe in here, there's light seeping in from between the buttons, i'm writing a story on his shirt, it's hard cos my pen is leaking and his body throbbing and twitching, i slip from under his coat: "can you give me a synonym for malicious?", "bitter, evil, spiteful, rancorous, resentful, malignant, mischievous...", "those aren't any good, nevermind", i slip under his coat again and use 'mischievous', cos it sounds playful and it rolled so smoothly from his tongue: 'misjeevas' he pronounced it, the story is not really a story, it's just what i did last night: "last night i went over to the kinky nightnurse, it was his night off, he was brushing his pony's tail when i arrived, his pony is moody and mischievous, i was wearing mediterranean scents, blue jeans and my favourite oasis t-shirt, i fed his pony poisonous berries and we went inside, straight to the first floor where his bedroom is, he tied me to the bed and blindfolded me, i held my eyes open, the cloth was prickly, he fucked me hard and afterwards he arsefucked me hard, he untied me, i removed the cloth, we downed a bottle of cheap calvados in front of his mirror, he looked gawky and vulnerable, i loathed him, i wanted to slit his throat with my stanley knife, but instead i moaned to him about my sheffielder angel whilst gloomily playing with myself, the kinky nightnurse kicked me out of the house, i checked on his pony, it was wheezing in a corner of the stable, i felt sorry for it, i hugged it tightly, its coat was caked with dried-up blood and mud, i tried to drag it out of the stable but it wouldn't move, 'stay here then and die a horrible death by your owner's callous hands, you miserable beast, you' i said and left the stable, i then took the..." i've run out of shirt, it doesn't matter, i politely ask the sweet gullible doctor if i can give him head, he has to think about it, "ok" he says after forty anxious seconds, i unzip his pants and suck his handsome boner, i swallow his cum, wipe my mouth with his sleeve and ask him if that lump on my nape is something to be worried about, i take his hand and put it on the lump, he rubs it, says that it's not a tumour and runs his finger down my spine, i suck his cock again in return for the diagnosis, and also because it's a mighty fine boner, i spit his spunk at the window of the book store, the sweet gullible doctor zips up his pants and says that he's got patients to see, "russian patients?" i ask, "some of them russian", "one-legged russian patients?", "none of them one-legged", the sweet gullible doctor walks away, an old dusty frenchman unlocks the book store, i get inside, read a few paraghraphs here, a few dreadful coastal poems there, i buy a dodgy scottish crime novel that's well thumbed and blood-stained, it smells of lavender and smoked heifers, the first chapter is a bit disappointing, but the second chapter sucks me in, and it's not until chapter six that i look up, sigh, and long for another boner.

I'M WALKING THE WALK BAREFOOT / hmm, i vaguely remember it, there was a hotel next to a german DIY store, it had a talking elevator with a slightly mancunian accent, i was there with my sheffielder angel, we listened to the kinks and i jerked him off, have you ever jerked off a sheffielder angel to "lola"? it's depressing, that's why i'm going over to my dodgy neighbour, again, he'll beat the gloom out of me right and proper, or maybe he'll shove it deeper, anyway, i put on my rags, paint my eyelids, siphon some of christopher's aftershave onto my collarbone, smoke a fag and leave my bedsit, i'm just gonna sit on my doorstep for a while, maybe i'll get chatted up by a chubby flemish vixen, the sun is setting, the chubby flemish vixens are ignoring me, i stub my fag out on the inside of my left knee and knock on my dodgy neighbour's door, he's not home, i sit myself on his doorstep, smoke a fag, maybe i'll get chatted up by a skinny mancunian crime writer, it's drizzling, there are no skinny mancunian crime writers in this wretched coastal town, well that's too bad, it's pouring, i take off my shoes, i put them on my dodgy neighbour's window sill, i don't like them, they smother my feet, i mean: a kinky flemish fishmonger bought them for me last wednesday after i'd so ferociously fondled the tip of his cock, every time i wear them they call me a "whore", i mean: they squeak and every squeak sounds like "whore", yesterday i went to wee andy's house, i was wearing them bloody shoes: "whore whore whore whore whore", i stopped, took them off and walked barefoot to wee andy's place, when i finally arrived at wee andy's there were 23 thorns, 36 glass splinters, 18 nails, 3 feathers from a sparrow's belly and 56 beetles stuck in my feet, wee andy washed them and tenderly plucked all that junk; my dodgy neighbour opens his garage and drives inside, i enter the garage, the door closes, my dodgy neighbour gets out of the car, grabs my tits and snogs me, "you're soaked, kitten", he drags me up the stairs and into the bathroom, he undresses me, wrings out my rags and hangs them over his bath tub, he pushes me against the sink and fingers me, "your minge is dry, kitten", he spits on his fingertips and tries again, i tug at my left lobe and purr, my neighbour drags me to the kitchen and pours me a glass of white south african wine, he sweeps it off the table and slaps me, "don't just sit there, kitten, clean it up", i get up, leave the kitchen, go to his bedroom, lie myself on his bed and count the worms in his wooden ceiling, i can't really see the worms, but i can see the holes from where they started burrowing, "284", my dodgy neighbour enters the bedroom, "284 what, kitten? shags? shots? cars? canes? crucifixes?", he chuckles and rubs my belly, "284 holes in your ceiling from where the worms started burrow...", "shut up, kitten", i unzip his pants and pull down his huge beige drawers, there are holes in the drawers through which sweat fumes can escape, i'm not gonna count them, there are too many, i tickle his cock with the tip of my tongue for a while and then take it deep, i suck it ferociously and swallow his cum, my dodgy neighbour pulls up his drawers, zips up his pants and drags me to the living room, he lifts me up and puts me on his flemish stove, "dance, kitten", the stove is hot, i'm jumping up and down, i try to jump off but my neighbour keeps pushing me back, after twenty minutes he puts me on the floor again, "that was a lame performance, kitten", i can't feel my soles, i sit myself on the floor and look at them, they look like overcooked reindeer loins, my neighbour pours some spanish rum on them and gives me the bottle, i take a swig, stagger to the bathroom, squeeze myself into my damp rags, i scowl at my distorted reflection in the tap, punch myself in the nose and leave the house, oh no, those fucking shoes are still standing on his window sill, i try to put them on, but they don't fit anymore, i clutch them and enter my bedsit, the illiterate rentboy is stuffing his face with canned canadian salmon, i show him my soles, he hugs me tightly and then shows me his.

ANOTHER BLOODY PRICELESS NIGHT / there's a minging russian hobo entering the barren car park of the disused theme park, the theme was bees, he's carrying a heavy bucket, i go over to him, i have to know what's in the bucket, it's blood, the hobo puts the bucket on a soapbox and sits himself on a piss-soaked checkered blanket, "whose blood is this??", "take a swig and maybe you'll guess", i dip my index finger into the bucket and lick off the blood, "a welsh taxidermist?", "no", "a mancunian heroin pusher?", "no", "a retarded flemish cook?", "no", "give me a clue", "no", i plunge my hand into the bucket and lick off the dark clotted blood, it tastes of petrol-soaked rabbit bowels and cheap brogues, stray dogs live on a diet of petrol-soaked rabbit bowels and cheap brogues, but then so do all the hobos, and so do christopher and i, "i know it! it's the blood of the scruffy seeing-eye stray dog of that supposedly blind dour german hobo who set your organ-grinding monkey on fire two winters ago", "such a fine monkey it was, so intelligent and so considerate...", "do i get a prize for having guessed it?", "you gave three wrong answers before you got it right", "oh come on, don't be so fucking stingy", "you can have the bucket of blood", i lift it up, it's way too heavy to carry it all the way to wee andy's house, i pour some blood on my sneakers and some on my blouse and some on a broken white cot that's standing in the middle of the car park, i balance the bucket on my head and leave the car park, there are fireworks in the north french sky, i trudge through derelict arcades and through sinister paddocks and through bleak dunes and through perv-infested parks and through ominous alleys and through glass-littered avenues and through cracked motorways and through disused rails and through sickly reservoirs and through looted supermarkets and through smouldering abattoirs and through the red light district and through abbeys where shady flemish crossbow guilds conspire and get out of their heads on coke and stout and skinny french vixens and through the drained swimming pool where the glue-sniffing underage bulgarian rentboys sniff and suck and doze, in the alley that's named after some flemish whore who once fed vincent van gogh scrambled eggs and absinthe-drenched boar cutlets i bump into the illiterate rentboy, "what's in the bucket?", i take the bucket and put it on the ground, "there's blood on your blouse, why is there blood on your blouse?", "i poured blood on my blouse", "why??", "because the bucket was too heavy", "why are you carrying along a bucket of blood? and whose blood is it??", "A. i don't know. B. guess", "you haven't killed anyone, have you?", "don't be daft, i couldn't kill a john to save myself, or maybe i could, but anyway, i got this bucket from a russian hobo, the one with the purple birthmark on his collarbone and the scissors tattooed on his right hand", "did he kill someone?", "don't be daft, he couldn't stab a german hobo to save himself, he killed a seeing-eye dog", "why did he catch its blood in a bucket??", "i don't know, christopher, does it matter?", the illiterate rentboy shrugs, we sit ourselves on a stubby brown doormat and smoke some fags, a flemish geezer passes and kicks the bucket, the blood merges with the dewy cobbles and disappears into the cracks, i pick the bucket up and run to wee andy's house, i knock on his door eagerly impatiently, wee andy opens the door, "there are blood stains on your blouse and sneakers", "i know!!", "what's happened? what's in the bucket?", "nothing", i fling the bucket at a parking meter and enter the house, "don't you want to know whose blood this is?", "whose blood is it?", "last night i was reading a russian article about obese black crack-addicted teen mums in bristol on the doorstep of a disused sweet shop, just minding my own business, when all of a sudden a nefarious glaswegian yuppie cunt snatched the article, tore it up, pulled out a kitchen knife and tried to stab me in the throat, i dodged 224 stabs, a minging russian hobo spotted the scene, he kicked the glaswegian geezer in the back, pulled out his dagger and stabbed him in the spleen, and then he turned on me!! i grabbed the kitchen knife and planted it in his paunch and frantically pushed and stirred for two hours, we dropped onto the pavement, we kissed and made up, he bled to death on top of me, but first he confessed to 58 rapes and 46 bribes, can i take a bath please?", "yeah sure, you know where it is", i'm sitting in the tub, my blouse and sneakers are floating around me, i remember that organ-grinding monkey, it used to wear a pink skirt and a straw hat, and it had to grind out mournful russian hymns.

P.S. THEY PUT HORSE TRANQUILIZERS IN THE MASHED POTATOES / i'm sitting on a mound of dead batteries in the dreary desolate otter-infested car park of the disused danish oscilloscope factory, "ill cop" is all what's left of the word, it makes more sense this way, i don't even know what an oscilloscope looks like, let alone what it's supposed to do, i'm writing a letter to wee andy, the wee daft twat's in the nuthouse, nothing exciting, just a depression, not even a manic one, a boring, can't be bothered to comb my hair one, he should have asked me, but oh no, he had to be all theatrical and slit his wrists whilst auditioning for the part of the villain in some pseudo burlesque poof play, the villain's a malicious welsh gardener, so when they handed andy the garden shears he mumbled his two lines, burst into tears and slashed his arms, and now the wee cunt's attached to a plump green device that shrieks when he coughs and crackles when he belches and whistles when i punch it, just because he left me in the lurch when i was having the time of my life in the nuthouse three years ago doesn't mean i have to do the same: "Dear Andy, cheer up for fuck's sake. how's the food? how are the pills? tell them motherly mustached nurses that there are prim catholic north french maidens in your head and that they're telling you to bludgeon your ponies to death with your glass coffee table and that they're calling you lewd and shallow and selfish, but sometimes at night they talk dirty and want you to jerk off your blind crippled psychotic demented alcoholic eighty-something roommate, they'll give you lithium and a separate room if you tell them that. i passed your house this morning, someone's broken all your windows!! have they taught you yet how to make a silk purse out of a reindeer's liver? are your fellow nutters gregarious or solitary? suicidal or manipulative? garrulous or muttering sordid confessions into their plastic cups? psychotic or faking it? anorexic or illiterate? traumatised or bragging about their incestuous relatives? gullible or cunning? perverts or whores? anyway, i just wanted to let you know that i'm well relieved that they didn't give you the part of the malicious welsh gardener, i'm also well relieved that you didn't bleed to death on that small ghastly stage under those harsh lights which didn't do much for your exquisite bone structure, nor for your handsome ribs, oh andy, why do you always have to be so suicidal the week before your father's birthday? tsk. last night i chatted up a kinky flemish fishmonger in the drab sinister dingo-infested car park of the disused mongolian oscillograph factory- what's an oscillograph??-, 'ill rap' is all that's left of the word though, it was the kinky flemish fishmonger who told me that it used to be an oscillograph factory and that his retarded brother 'disappeared into the cogs five years ago', sounds pretty horrible, doesn't it? we walked to his place, his place was a tiny musty flat above a derelict chinese restaurant, he sat himself on a green stool in the middle of the living room and gloomily angrily wolfed down ten rhubarb stalks, there were no chairs, i sat myself on his television and watched him, i turned on the television, it vibrated so violently i had to clutch the buttons not to fall on the floor, i listened to the daft dialogues of a vulgar german soap, and then the fishmonger finally dragged me off his television and into his bedroom, i unzipped his pants, took out his big bad boner and sucked it EXTRA FEROCIOUSLY, he lamely bit my tits for a while and then he fingered me, which was nice enough, he entered me and came between my tits, he gave me a pink handkerchief that was adorned with frisky yellow rabbits to wipe the spunk off my chest, i wanted to give the handkerchief back but he bellowed: 'keep it', so i kept it, and this morning i washed it in my shower tray, two hours ago i blew my nose with it, and an hour ago i waved christopher goodbye with it, just like in a film, i was standing on a smut-stained bleak platform and the illiterate rentboy kissed my hand and hopped onto the train just in time and yelled: "don't forget to tell my mancunian pimp that i'm..." and then the doors closed and the train left, and only fifteen minutes ago i wiped the petrol and blood off the broken face of a dead russian hobo with it. come back, miserable cunt. whatever you do: don't fall in love with the kinky nightnurse. love, Delphine", i jump off the mound, an avalanche unfurls and smothers 22 otters, i post the letter and suck the petrol out of my handkerchief.

HOT SUICIDE / there's this dodgy geezer on the other end of the suicide hotline, he wants me to describe the colours of my nipples, and i would if i wasn't colour-blind; i don't really want to kill myself and he doesn't really want to talk people out of killing themselves, so let's call it even and meet up after your shift, where are you anyway? and do you get paid for chatting up suicidal orphan girls? he'll pick me up in brussels at five am, in the alley next to the most ghastly brothel in the world that's quite inappropriately called "eden", these brothel geezers aren't very inventive, every red light district i visit i always come across the same names, paradisio, eden, beverly hills or temptation; eden it is then, or at least the piss-soaked alley next to eden, i guess it's close enough; i take the train to brussels and i feel all fidgety and i'm tingling with anticipation, i'm wearing my favourite turkoise knickers, my mobile phone's ringing, this wonderwall ringtone sounds better than the actual song, no it doesn't, it's the retarded flemish cook, i'm quite attached to him now, and not just financially, he's just so harmless, i can never decide whether to hug him or punch him, he wants to know where i am: "i'm on a train to brussels, i'm about to get raped by some dodgy geezer who chats up orphan girls on the suicide hotline... hey, wasn't that how we got to know each other??!!" of course it wasn't, i'm only baiting the retard; i met him at the nuthouse, he was one of the more endearing nutters, totally self-obsessed nonetheless; he's blubbering, so i break the connection; there's a spiteful busker on the train but it's not my father, he's got an awfully whingey nasal voice, he's very good looking, but it hardly redeems him, he's singing about cold war and prostitution, about russian whores really, "would you stop your whingeing? i don't wanna know how or when you were cruelly rejected by tatiana's gorgeous tits", the spiteful busker just ignores me and continues whining about svetlana's treacherous thighs and whatnot, thankfully the next stop is mine, the station is deserted apart from a few hobos, but i don't think they're alive anyway cos they're cold and blue and when i tug at their sleeves they just fall down like cardboard action figures, well like cardboard at least, their black dog is emaciated, i take it with me, no actually it follows me, a few strokes and these poor deprived orphan creatures never leave you, until they find someone who strokes them better that is; the dodgy geezer is standing next to his red pimp car, "no dog in my car", "are you talking about me or him?", "i'm talking about the skinny flea-infested four-legged creature", "i take it that's me then", "NO,THAT", and he points at my new friend, the poor thing is trembling, i take it in my arms and i walk away, away from that cruel cold-hearted dodgy geezer who chats up suicidal orphan girls and called me a dog; the first shops are opening, i buy us some breakfast, the dog and i are sitting on a piss-saturated doorstep spitting at the conceited junkie scum and their fur-clad bitches that smugly parade in front of us, it's a beautiful morning, brussels is looking sleazy but inviting, the black dog is resting its weary head on my knee, all that hobo hysteria must have cost him some hair, he's got bald patches on his back and belly, we roam the streets, i realise that my dog hasn't got a name yet, we pass a library and the windows are displaying fucking insipid middle class yankee novels by fucking unimaginative over-privileged neurotic yankee writers, one of them is wearing a white suit, it's that tom wolfe geezer again, i burn down the library and i name the dog "arson".

I WANTED TO SAVE HIM,NOT BREAK HIS BACK / i'm visiting wee andy at the nuthouse, there are a lot of familiar faces, the same sad rape victims festering in their self-pity, the usual alcoholic reprobates with their usual tales of former glories, the bloody deprived junkies terrorising the discontented underpaid staff who are only in it for the traumatised fanny and the fucked-up indie boys, there are the demented old tarts tied to their beds, choking on their food, which is probably the only reason why they get fed at all; "i stick out like a sore thumb in this place", "sticking out like a sore thumb in a nuthouse really isn't something you should feel too sad about, wee deluded cunt", "if you've only come here to throw abuse at me, you can fuck right off", "oooh, i see someone's been brainwashed by those well-meaning therapists", "they tell me i shouldn't hang out with you any more, that i should drop you, they told me that our friendship's abusive", "maybe you should think for yourself", "i do like you, delphine", "and i like you", "then why did you set my house on fire?", "are you still going on about that?! it wasn't anything personal, i was destroying a symbol, it could have been any ugly middle class cage", "yes, but that ugly middle class cage happened to be my home", "so now you're making the nuthouse your new home, you haven't really bettered yourself, have you?", "i thought these nutters were your friends?", "i'll just ignore that, no actually i won't ignore that, some of these nutters i befriended when i stayed here, but they're all gone now, either dead or roaming ghastly streets you wouldn't even walk in the daytime; the ones who are still here, still supposedly traumatised about the exact same things they moaned about five years ago, them i loathe, they're the living dead, don't join them, wee scared cunt, i'm sure we can work this out", "do you have a house for me then?", "don't be so fucking greedy, you can stay at my bedsit", "why would i wanna do that?", "yes, why would you? when you can get all the sympathy and pills in the world right here?", "exactly", "by the way, have you met the kinky nightnurse yet?", "yes", "and?", "and what?", "did he brutally arsefuck you and force you to lick demented fanny?" wee andy just shrugs, "that's it, we're out of here, i'll provide you with sympathy and pills, well no, not sympathy, but pills should do, come on, pack your things", but the wee apathetic cunt doesn't move from his bed, so i pack his stuff for him, he's looking at me and then he starts sobbing, "what the fuck is wrong with you?!!", "i'll miss the nightnurse, i kinda fancy him", "yeah yeah yeah, we all fancied him in the beginning, but then we snapped out of it and realised he'd beaten, raped, humiliated, mutilated and tortured us for two years, and we'll bloody well never get those years back, so get over him, it's not like he's the only kinky cunt in the world, if you so desperately want to be brutally arsefucked and tied and beaten, i suggest you ask christopher for his directory, look under the 'g', lots of pervs seem to have names that start with a 'g', yes that's their first name, nobody gives their last name to a rentboy, but what about our friendship?", "what about it?", "isn't it abusive enough?", "it is", "then why look for kinky cunts?", "i am not looking for kinky cunts, i only said that i'm gonna miss the nightnurse", "and a slap on your wrists for repeating it, you wee insensitive cunt", "sorry", "let's get out of here", "but how?", "through the window", "i'm afraid of heights", "now is really not the time to give in to your silly fears, come on, jump on my back and close your eyes, it'll all be over soon", i slide down a huge rainpipe with the wee trembling cunt on my back, it makes awkward noises and for a minute i think it's gonna crack, but then we're on the roof , from here i can already catch a glimpse of freedom three stories beneath us, we take a little break, i drink a bottle of wine, which probably isn't very sensible considering i have to carry the wee traumatised cunt over all those narrow ledges and i always get so fucking reckless when i'm drunk, even more so than normal, but then recklessness has never seriously hurt me before, i down another bottle and then we resume our expedition, well i resume, the wee cunt is merely trembling and sobbing on my back, his tears are trickling on my nape, trickling down my spine, or maybe it's my sweat, it doesn't matter, we're almost on the ground, this is the tricky part though, the last story, no rainpipes, no ladders, not even window sills or cracks between crumbling stones, there are no crumbling stones, only this huge smooth facade that harbours all those bloody patronising middle class twats with all their useless degrees and gravy-stained ties, i'm gonna have to jump, wee andy breaks my fall, sadly there was nobody to break wee andy's fall, he's not breathing, there are people running out of the nuthouse, uniformed pigs, nurses, doctors, i quickly run away, when i'm at a safe distance i turn around, they're carrying the wee oversensitive cunt inside, i feel gutted, story of my life: i come so fucking close to saving a sweet fragile indie boy and then i ruin it by crushing him.

I DON'T CARE FOR FRAIL FLEMISH PEASANTS,I DON'T CARE FOR THEIR MILK AND I DON'T CARE FOR THEIR SQUIRRELS / i am roaming the bleak flat flemish countryside, all the cattle and hirsute peasants are inside cos it's freezing, or maybe everyone's dead and i'm the only person left in this world, but probably not, cos only five minutes ago i bumped into a sleazy polish priest, he was combing the bleak flat flemish countryside for underage gullible orphan girls, i thought that i was safe since i'm neither underage nor gullible, but he yanked my arm and dragged me into a wee and hardly ominous forest, his cock was also wee and hardly ominous, but he had two gigantic fists and he shoved one up my arse and with the other he banged my chest, i said to him: "please don't kill me, i don't want to die on my mother's birthday", "what care i for your bloody mother's birthday?" he snapped and snogged me, i then said: "another reason why you can't kill me today is that there's an unfinished story lying in my shower tray, and i've finally found an appropriate ending, and i'd feel really gutted if it went to waste", "what care i for your bloody unfinished story?" he shrieked and shoved his fist deeper, i got pretty desperate then, i said: "there's an illiterate rentboy living in my wardrobe, he's too gloomy to comb his hair, he's too lazy to wash his socks, he's too illiterate to sign petitions and he's too greedy to decline awkward offers from kinky flemish clerics, he needs me", the sleazy polish priest pulled his fist out of my arse and stopped banging my chest, he clutched a sickly shrub and shooed me away, but now i'm all alone, i can hear shots in the distance though, and whimpering pheasants, it's not really my mother's birthday today, i haven't really found an appropriate ending either, but what i said about christopher is true, i am tired of roaming, i knock on the broad green door of a sinister cottage, a frail bespectacled peasant opens the door: "good afternoon sir, could i have a glass of skim milk and a bowl of oxtail soup, please?", "sure, come in", i sit myself at a small plastic table in the kitchen, there's a silvery squirrel in a cage on his flemish stove, "can i stroke your squirrel?" it's not a metaphor this time, "i wouldn't if i was you, it's in a foul mood today", "i'm good with rodents", "suit yourself", the skinny peasant is polishing a brass kettle, i open the cage and put my hand in it, the vicious rodent bites my thumb and hisses at me, i pull my hand away and scowl at the demented squirrel, the peasant tenderly and patiently disinfects and bandages my thumb, it makes me drowsy, it makes me think i'm falling in love: "you don't look like a flemish peasant at all, you look like a welsh crime writer", the flemish peasant blushes and mumbles something apologetic, i wolf down three bowls of oxtail soup and down two pints of spanish rum, the psychotic squirrel has wrapped its tail around its puny body and is snoring, i tell the peasant about that sleazy polish priest, "foreigners, tsk tsk tsk" is all he says, that's not even a proper sentence, i was hoping he'd stroke my chest and whisper some flemish comfort in my ear, "i was hoping you'd stroke my chest", "if that's what you want", "that's what i want, and what i want even more is to stroke your squirrel, if you know what i mean", he knows what i mean, he leads me to his cold musty bedroom and undresses me slowly and politely, "don't be so fucking polite, rip them off, like this", i rip off my blouse and bra, he snorts, coughs and then finally starts fondling my tits, i unzip his pants and touch his cock, it twitches, i take it in my mouth and suck it, on his night table are smug russian novels and a fibre batman figure, i swallow his cum, we sit on the bed and smoke some fags, he covers my body with a checkered blanket, i shrug it off, i fondle my nipples and tell him about my dodgy neighbour's crossbows, "sometimes he locks me up in his garage and then i have to polish his crossbows all night long, and the beeswax stings my eyes, and i trip over arrows and sprain my ankle all the time, that's why i walk with a slight limp, and sometimes i nod off and dream about my unfinished stories, and the next morning my dodgy neighbour examines all the crossbows and if they're not properly polished then he drags me up the stairs into his attic and ties me to a worm-infested wooden pillar and fucks and maims me with his austrian cutlery, so far i've never succeeded in properly polishing them all, there are so many, you've no idea", the frail flemish peasant stubs his cigarette out on the mattress, pats my chest, bites my nipples, mumbles something kinky or sweet, and shoves his fingers into my cunt.

BASHING SEXY GEORGE AND BAITING WEE ANDY / "yesterday we bashed sexy george", "who?", "you know, the old drunkard who only wears pyjamas and a green cap and who stands in his doorway all day and night", "oh, what did you do that for? he's a nice guy", "why don't you suck his cock if he's such a nice guy, wee boring middle class twat", wee andy just sighs, "we pelted him with oranges and dead pigeons, he was well mad, he called us dirty little slags, and then we tried to snog him but he got really aggressive and he nearly throttled me", "was christopher there?", "no, the miserable poof had locked himself in my bedsit and was wanking over liam pics, it was just me and two crazy orphan girls, it was a great night, there were lots of posh cars passing through our street and the corporate pigs inside the cars were scowling at us, looking all smug and scornful, so we threw sticks and stones at their big immaculate fuckawful cars, and they got out, but angie, that's the orphan girl who killed her mum, she pulled out a huge kitchen knife and jumped on the hood of their cars and did a little dance while nathalie and me, we squealed like tortured rodents, and the middle class cunts all looked totally terrified, which was hilarious, for all their money and all their bourgeois scum friends in high places they can't even stand up to three skinny orphan girls, ha", "that's awful", "i should have known that a wee unimaginative middle class cunt like yourself would take it up for them bloody corporate pigs rather than for his best friend, pfffff, you're just jealous, you're just a wee frustrated cunt in a wheelchair, just be grateful that i'm here to tell you about the fireworks, it's the closest to mayhem you'll ever get", wee andy's rolling his eyes, "i brought you some britpop records", "no one cool listens to britpop", "you think cool people wear sunglasses", "yeah", "fucking shallow poof", i put on the lightning seeds just to bait the wee pedantic cunt and it's quite frankly fuckawful, there's an organ, a mellotron and strings in this song and singing about the milky way and about dolphins and about colliding with pervs and about adopting skinny orphan girls, but i'm sure i'm mishearing the lyrics, wee andy reckons this song's about cold war, what a deluded tosser, he thinks that every indie song's either about cold war or prostitution, "no, i don't, i think that every indie song SHOULD BE about either cold war or prostitution", "and why's that, you wee deluded indie snob?", "i don't know, ask nicky wire", "you're so full of shit, and you got it all wrong, every indie song should be about either class war, skinny orphan girls, obsessive stalking, cocksucking or alcoholism", "that sums up your life pretty accurately", "cheeky cunt... i wish you'd been there last night, don't you ever feel the urge to pelt middle class scum with oranges or to bash demented old drunkards??!", "no", "can't i convert you?", "no", "you wee ungrateful cunt, others would jump at the opportunity", "at the opportunity to bash demented old drunkards?", "with three skinny orphan girls", "i'm sure they would", "you're sure they would what?", "JUMP AT THE OPPORTUNITY", "i knew that, i was only trying to wind you up", "i wish you were a little more considerate, my back hurts, rehabilitation is a bitch and i'm fed up with sitting in a wheelchair, so you might wanna be a little nicer", "pfffff, an over-privileged middle class cunt in a wheelchair is still an over-privileged middle class cunt, and i don't feel sorry for you, if anything, i loathe you even more now, you can't even wear your wound with pride", "harsh", "harsh but true", "is christopher gonna visit me today?", "no, you wee sentimental cunt, christopher's never gonna visit you, he's a selfish greedy opportunist rentboy and he doesn't give a fuck about anyone, get over it", "i thought you liked him", "that doesn't mean i can't see him for what he is, i like you as well, that doesn't mean i can't see you for the wee unimaginative oversensitive middle class cunt you are", "cheers, delph", "don't call me delph, wee rude cunt", "why not?", "it sounds dodgy", "i thought you liked dodgy", "shut up", which is exactly what the wee pouty cunt does, "stop scowling at me, wee oversensitive cunt," but the wee surly cunt just continues scowling until i pelt him with the fruit that's lying on his night table, the wee treacherous cunt pushes the alarm button and i get thrown out of the hospital by two sturdy security geezers, at the corner of the street i turn around, wee andy's looking out of his window, i think he's sobbing, i throw kisses at him and he just shakes his head wearily.

A RAMBLING SLANDERING COCKSUCKING EMERGENCY / i am rubbing myself against my dodgy neighbour's tinsel tap, tinsel tap is not a metaphor for limp boner, i don't do metaphors, i do crassness, i also do crack and self harm, sometimes i do hopelessness, but don't get me started on that, it's not very uplifting: the tap is warm and when i come i think about that new year's eve that i spent with the retarded flemish cook two years ago, it was both magical and dreadful, i fucked his cancerous bedridden mother, i fucked three dead lobsters, i fucked the retarded flemish cook into a more blissful state of idiocy, i drank myself into a very crooked frame of mind, i snorted myself into believing that i was a fucking great coastal poet, then eventually new year's day came and punched all those delusions of grandeur and tragic personalities out of my fucking unreliable mind, but some of those personalities are still up there and they torment me, at least that's what i tell my sweet gullible doctor; my dodgy neighbour enters the bathroom: "daddy's here to wash your minge", he takes a fluffy yellow budgie-shaped washing glove out of a drawer, puts it on and drops his hand in the water, he's caressing my minge, i can't come underwater, i get out of the water, my neighbour fingers me gently, i can't come when i'm wet, i dry myself with a huge red towel, my neighbour is brushing my hair, i open the drawer where he keeps all his razor blades, i pick one that has a smooth dark blue handle, i make two long deep cuts on my left arm, one gash looks a bit like that run over hare i scraped off the north french motorway yesterday, the other gash looks like a foaming volcano, "i'm getting fed up with this, kitten, if you want attention just strip off your clothes and do your funny little dance on my german table", my neighbour pours red disinfectant on my lovely gashes and rudely bandages my arm with a musty tablecloth, i think it's austrian cos there's edelweiss embroidered on it, i feel delightfully light-headed, i'm aching for my next gash though, "i'm aching for a fuck", my dodgy neighbour carries me into his tiny immaculate bedroom and licks the grotesque gash i was born with, i'm not very fond of it, but my neighbour is, he licks it with admirable devotion and glee, when i come i think about that new year's eve that i spent with my sheffielder angel three years ago, i tripped over a wire and fell against his aquarium, it smashed onto the floor, all his tropical fish were flapping and shrieking, i was flapping and shrieking too, the broken glass had cut my calves and chest, i filled the sink with his bourbon and threw the fish in it, i was confused, all those gorgeous creatures died, we buried them in the deserted car park of the disused seafood factory on new year's day, my stitches burst when i knelt to pray; my dodgy neighbour drags me into his living room, we watch a german documentary about japanese mobsters, i rip off the tablecloth and study the gashes, they're dormant, they've stopped bleeding, wee andy says that i shouldn't brag about my gashes, just because he hasn't got the guts nor self-disgust to slash his arms, pfff, bloody ignorant over-privileged twat, my neighbour pushes me down onto the couch and bites my nipples, he fingers me for forty minutes but i'm too drowsy to come, i clutch his big flemish nose, close my eyes and think about the dolphin friendly tuna tins that the illiterate rentboy compulsively shoplifts and stuffs our shower tray with.

SECOND ATTEMPT,SECOND BROKEN BACK / "do you remember the first time we met?", "aye", "could you sound a wee bit more enthusiastic, you wee rude middle class twat?" but wee andy just shrugs, i think they put him on new medication, he's always been a wee miserable poof but today he's totally apathetic, "you're no exciting company", "well i guess you'll just have to be exciting for the both of us", "as usual", "as usual", "or yeah, you could just echo me, that should make for interesting conversation, wee miserable middle class twat", "hasn't the psychiatrist warned you that you couldn't throw abuse at me anymore?", "do i look like i give a fuck about what some up-tight middle class shrink tells me?", "it hurts, you know", "what does?", "the abuse", "oh don't be so fucking self-indulgent, you know i mean well, you bloody ungrateful cunt", "do you mean well? i wonder about that sometimes, i sometimes wonder why you're so angry and i wonder why i put up with it", "i can tell that the well-meaning little therapists have proper fucked with your head, you're not supposed to analyse our friendship, wee over-privileged middle class cunt, just be grateful to have such a loyal friend", "'loyal or obsessive?", "oh would you shut up, wee cheeky cunt, and fetch me some painkillers", but wee andy just shakes his head wearily as if i've just asked him for something outrageous, pffff, the wee stingy cunt won't even share his pills, and i bloody well would do anything for him, that's fucking gratitude for you, typical middle class behaviour, those bloody middle class twats spit in the faces of their saviours, and this wee cunt is no exception to the rule, "i brought a few records i thought you might want to hear, joy division, super furry animals, ash and primal scream, wow i've got great taste in music", "cheers, delphine", "no need to get so excited, it's only rock'n'roll", "yeah", "boy, you need to get out of here before you fester in your bloody self-pity, you wee listless cunt, i'll help you escape", "i just got out of that wheelchair, i don't feel like having my back broken again, to be honest, i don't think i'd survive, it does still hurt a lot", "have some faith in me, you wee pessimistic drama queen", "i'm still going through rehab", "wow that sounds so cool, you're such a big rock'n'roll star, aren't you?", "its not that kind of rehab, besides, even if it was, it'd still not be cool", "bloody moralist twat", the wee cunt rolls his eyes, "oh don't be so fucking harsh, i wont fuck up this time, just hop on my back and we'll be on the ground before you can say vacuum cleaner", "nicky wire, eh?", "aye, you know me well, wee smart cunt", "i don't know why i let you talk me into this crazy stuff", "because you bloody well know i'm the only person in your smug safe middle class life who provides you with some proper entertainment", "entertainment, eh? just make sure you don't break my back this time", "shut your gob and jump on my back", which is exactly what the wee miserable poof does, i'm well prepared this time, took a few climbing lessons, well no admittedly i didn't, but boy, do i feel like a fucking alpinist, a fearless mountaineer, a bloody invincible explorer, you catch my drift, i feel fucking immortal and i owe it all to that bottle of rum, the wee pathetic cunt is trembling as we descend the stories, it's fucking nerve-wracking, it's hard enough as it is, but you try descending a nuthouse with a wee trembling poof clung to your back, its tricky, i'll tell you that much, we're almost on the ground, six more stories, hmm, wouldn't it be funny if i just climbed back up into his room, just for a laugh, but no, i can't be bothered, the wee middle class cunt has gained some weight, "have you been eating dead animals, you wee bloody salad dodger?!" but the wee bourgeois cunt doesn't answer, i'm thinking about whining heifers awaiting their horrendous execution, knowing full well they'll get killed, slamming their beautiful heads against their cages in a vain attempt to end their misery themselves, but it's no use, those bloody merciless human beings always get there first, poor innocent creatures, and just as i'm thinking about all this mammal misery i catch some bourgeois cunt on the third floor stuffing meat into his hideous mouth, i swing my fists at him, realising too late that i'm letting go of the wall and i'm bloody well falling and crushing wee andy's back again, exactly like he said i would.

DON'T DOWN THE DREGS / it doesn't really matter that my last savings and all my unfinished stories are stolen, i'm lying in bed with a blond flemish vixen and i'm kissing her tanned buttocks and it's hard to be cross when kissing such soft flesh, the rain is clattering against hollow pipes and fibre sheep and garden furniture, she's sliding her middle finger inside my cunt and licking my tits, this morning i was stacking dented dolphin-safe tuna tins, i was wearing ugly dark blue pants, a baggy dark blue sweater and a curry-yoghurt-ketchup-mustard-custard-chili-peanut butter-pineapple jam-stained apron, i was hating my distorted reflection on the lids and in the blade of my stanley knife, i wanted to maim her, maybe even kill her, but when i looked down, there at the bottom of my ladder stood my gorgeous blond colleague whose guts i hated until today, i always hate people's guts until they start talking to me, when our callous boss caught us chatting he bawled us out and sent us to the beer dungeon, we sat ourselves on a crate and downed the dregs of stout beers, the sorting machine sounded like a whimpering spaniel so i turned it off, all we heard then were the crap eighties songs the supermarket stereo relentlessly churns out, and the sound of breaking glass, i tried to slash my face with a broken bottle of dark leffe but the blond bitch stopped me, after two hours i knew too many embarrassing things about her father-in-law's heart and genitals, and the mounds of beer bottles were all still there, ominous and bloody tantalising, so we crawled through narrow ventilation systems and slid down hot pipes and nearly drowned in the ghastly reservoir where they raise and overfeed the supermarket salmon, i was relieved when we finally found the exit, the flemish bitch moaned about the weather, it was raining you see, flemish bitches always have to moan about the weather, we walked to her place, we didn't talk, i buried my repulsive face in the furry collar of her coat, when we walked through a dreary coastal street that was called cavalry i sniggered and told her about my sheffielder angel who saved me out of the claws of a perverted mancunian priest last night and she asked if she could borrow him, i said "fuck off, find yourself yer own sheffielder angel, slut"; we drank a lot of rum before we went to her bedroom cos she's self-conscious and frigid and i wasn't gonna make the first move, i was relieved though when she finally started rubbing my thighs; when i come her sickly black poodle pisses on the floor, i suggest we smother it with a pillow or at least throw it out the window, but she just shakes her pretty blond head and continues licking my throbbing cunt, the sickly black poodle is snapping at my calves, i push the two bitches off me and get dressed, i run out of the house and take the bus to the library, i can't believe i let that minging flemish slapper touch my cunt, bah; i pull out my black marker and write a story on the seat in front of me, i'm quite embarrassed about it when it's finished cos it's vulgar and spiteful and self-indulgent and there's a talking sea cow in it, i black it out and start again, but i'm too cross to write a decent story, i get off at the library, i sit myself in the lavatory with a dodgy scottish crime novel but i can't focus, i throw the novel in the sink and wash my hands ten thousand times; my reflection in the tiles is hazy, i punch her in the nose and break my right hand, i write a story on the mirror, but it's hard cos i'm not naturally left-handed and i'm still so very angry, a flemish bitch enters the lavatory, she frowns at my sentences, when the bitch is in her cubicle i slander her on all the walls; outside the churlish coastal sun is setting, it's cold and i wish i had a flemish girl to warm myself at, she can even have a sickly black poodle if she must, i comb the coastal streets for flemish vixens, but all creatures i bump into have testicles, the closest i get to a flemish vixen is here, on the lap of a fibre flemish slapper who's welcoming pervs and strangers to this seedy coastal restaurant in an affected nasal voice.

YOU'RE ALMOST AS ROTTEN AND TWISTED AS JESUS / the church doors are wide open, inviting me in, provoking me more like it, i go inside, my scalpel clenched in my fist, so tightly clenched that there's blood seeping through the cracks, i'm heavily armed, i've got black paint with me, brushes, a baseball bat, a screwdriver, two hammers, a mortar hoe, an axe, a rifle, a carving knife, nails, barbed wire and my favourite pair of scissors; they're nicely stacked in my backpack, the one i always use when i trash churches, schools, museums, restaurants, libraries, slaughterhouses, supermarkets and all those bloody houses where rotten twisted adults raise their children on a diet of meat and incest; my backpack is nicely decorated with oasis badges cos sometimes i just need that little push from my mancunian brothers; today i don't need no fucking push, i'm seething with anger and it's nothing to do with the catholic church but i'm gonna take it out on her anyway, the catholic church bloody well is female, it's like a mother who slams your head against radiators and breaks your nose with her bare fist and manages to make YOU feel guilty about it, the guilt i have long shrugged off, so now i can spend the rest of my life taking gleefully careless revenge, i'm no slave to the revenge, i revel in it but i'm not addicted to it, despite what wee andy says, but what does that wee cunt know anyway? he's spent half of his life gyrating like a spazwit and the other half, the first half, he spent spoilt pampered hugged kissed adored encouraged protected listened to, they put him on a fucking pedestal, they all thought he was the bee's knees, them deluded teachers, all his relatives, his friends, loving him, some even in awe; i never was in awe for that wee cunt, and i bullied him and i destroyed his paintings until the wee cunt was in awe with me, or in shock rather; so that wee cunt really is in no position to judge me, he's been living in a trap, and sure it was a cosy trap, but it still was a trap, i was never trapped cos i never relied on those rotten twisted adults, no matter how hard they hit me i never cringed or cowered, i fucking well gave them my smug defiant look and it made them froth with anger and they tried to kick and punch that look off my face, but they never succeeded cos i thought they were sad, sick and embarrassing and i knew i'd never grow up to become like them, this realisation filled me with self-confidence and this fucking tenacity that irks the world at large cos the world at large is lazy and complacent, boy do i sound arrogant, noel would be proud of me, and no wee andy is gonna stop me from trashing churches or burning down libraries, and all the wee bloody moralists better watch their back cos i've got a scalpel and it's eager; there's a man sitting in the front of the church, he's weeping, i take a seat next to him, a harsh uninviting cold dour seat i should add, "my son died last week in a car accident", "you miserable cunt, you'd really make anything up to get the minge, wouldn't you?", "WHAT??? my son, he died in a car accident", "yeah, yeah, yeah, and now you want a good old-fashioned shag to comfort you, right?" but he just shrugs, fucking ungrateful cunt, i put a hand on his thigh, he takes my hand and kisses it, "you're sweet, you're sweet, you're so sweet", "no, i'm not sweet, you deluded tosser, i laughed at your son's death for fuck's sake, how sweet is that?" but the old cunt's not listening, he's unzipping my jeans and sliding his fat hairy fingers into my cunt, "you're not wearing any knickers!!", "why would i bother wearing knickers when they're only gonna get devoured by rotten twisted adults?!" and the smart cunt says "hygiene", "if you're so worried about hygiene then what's your tongue doing down my cunt, fucking perv?" but he just shrugs as rotten twisted adults shrug when they've been caught being inconsistent and unreliable and licking out your cunt; the old fart bores me, i can't come, jesus is looking down on me with this air of superiority and contempt, the bloody arrogant cunt looks so self-righteous and so harsh and so unforgiving and so dour and so austere, SO FUCKING COLD AND CRUEL, i just want to rip my hair out and slaughter him, he's bloody well looking down on me, who does he think he is?? i hate you, jesus, i hate you, i hate you, i hate you, you're totally unreliable, you lying piece of scum, you're a rotten twisted adult, there's nothing comforting about your silly opinions and dodgy one-liners, i wish you would be resurrected so i could shove weeding hoes up your arse and carve oasis lyrics on your emaciated body and i would nail you to the gate of the slaughterhouse and that'll teach you!! but the supposedly mourning father doesn't give a fuck about my despair, he completely ignores my rage, he's not even slightly bemused, pffffff, what an unimaginative thick cunt, doesn't he realise that my rant's aimed at all rotten twisted adults? and he's arsefucking me on the altar and his son died a week ago in a car accident and he's shoving candles up my arse, the same fucking candles he lit an hour ago to conjure his supposed grief, and he doesn't care for my oasis badges, so clearly this is a good example of a total rotten twisted adult, not yet as rotten and twisted as jesus, but getting there.

TODAY I'M A GERMAN CHAMBERMAID / my dodgy neighbour and i are smoking fags and listening to the radio in the grey volvo in his garage, the engine's running but we won't choke cos there's an ingenious device attached to the ceiling, it's orange and it sucks up smoke and spits it into the chimney, my dodgy neighbour isn't suicidal, i don't usually like people who aren't suicidal, but i like him cos he's so blatantly sleazy and it takes guts to be sleazy in a small catholic coastal town, actually i loathe him, but time passes so much quicker when i pretend i don't, "i love you", "don't be so fucking sentimental, old tart", "i'm not old", "you're very fucking old compared to my twelve year old bulgarian vixen", i'm wearing the clothes of the german chambermaid my neighbour was married to for five years fifty years ago, i feel big and awkward in these clothes, my dodgy neighbour wants me to cry for help in german when he punches me in the face, "hilfe", "say it with more passion", he punches me in the stomach, "hilfe", he scratches my nipples with his wristwatch, "hilfe", he turns off the engine and the radio, gets out of the car, walks over to his work table and pats his crossbows fatherly, he picks one up, comes to me, throws it on my lap: "this one weighs more than you, kitten", i push it off me and smoke another fag, he drags me out of the car, rips off the stiff black skirt and rubs his limp cock against my thighs, "hilfe", i stroke the tip of his cock with my thumb, "hilfe", he cums on my knees, pulls up his ghastly drawers, zips up his pants, grabs my wrist and pushes me up the stairs into his living room, i turn on the radio, there's a melancholic italian song playing, "hilfe", it reminds me of the august day that wee andy and i wasted by moaning about the illiterate rentboy's foul moods and fickle behaviour, the ice cream van passed wee andy's house 38 times that day, this is the song it was playing through a chrome-coloured device attached to the roof, 38 fucking times, wee andy bought strawberry ice cream twice, the second time he tripped over shears and dropped it, a gloomy alsatian apathetically licked it off the pavement, my dodgy neighbour unbuttons my white blouse, folds it, puts it on his coffee table, undoes my bra and squeezes my tits mechanically, "my sheffielder angel has a scottish girlfriend who...", "has stars tattooed all over her minge blah blah blah", that's not what i was gonna say actually, i was gonna say: 'has designed a fucking atrocious book jacket for the newest english translation of crime and punishment', but yes, she has stars tattooed all over her minge, i know cos we once shared a bath at my sheffielder angel's place cos he's stingy, and i quite like taking baths with girls to be honest, but she was prim and pale and she slapped my hand when i sisterly stroked her left tit, "what are you thinking of, kitten?", "of the berlin big wheel", my dodgy neighbour pushes me down onto his couch, shoves two pillows under my buttocks and starts licking my minge, "hilfe", i shudder and come and sneeze, i put the german chambermaid's clothes back on and pour myself a pint of bourbon, i down it, there is sand and glass stuck in my throat, i take a swig from a bottle of cheap spanish rum, my dodgy neighbour snatches the bottle away from me: "you've had enough, kitten", he undresses me, i turn off the radio and face him, he's got ugly ruddy meaty cheeks, thin brownish lips, bloodshot eyes and a purple wart on his left temple, i snog him and fondle his balls, he throws me on the floor, fetches a cucumber from the fridge and shoves it up my arse, "hilfe", "shut up, bitch, it's not funny anymore", he punches me in the lungs and licks my buttocks, "hilfe... i mean: help", he bangs my head against his coffee table for ten minutes, he gives me back my jeans and oasis t-shirt, i put them on and pour myself another pint of bourbon, "you can leave if you want, kitten", but i don't leave, i stay and watch a russian documentary about north american beavers with him.

I DON'T YARN, I SPIN / i am spinning wee andy's plates on five sticks, they are nice plates, homely, old-fashioned, elegant austrian flowers painted on their rims, not that you can see them now that they whirl so rapidly, i am holding two sticks in my hands, balancing one on my head, the fourth is standing on my left shoulder, and my right toes are clutching the fifth, wee andy's gone out to buy a new plastic mate for his goldfish and fags and checkered napkins, he'll be so impressed with me, i've always known that i was made for the circus, i was born to spin plates on sticks stark naked whilst singing oasis songs, it was an armenian wine merchant who taught me this last night, i befriended him on a piss-soaked bench in the park where i once befriended a mancunian playwright who taught me how to ride poodles and how to jump through fiery hoops, or at least how to make them poodles jump through fiery hoops, but that's a different story, one that has a rather blood-soaked and tear-stained ending i should add, but anyway, the armenian wine merchant sat himself next to me, he offered me mints, i declined them, they ruin my taste buds, he offered me a swig from his bottle of flemish geneva, i declined that too cos there were thistles and nails on the bottom of the bottle, thankfully he also had a flask of bourbon with him, i gratefully eagerly accepted and downed it, it made me paranoid though, or maybe just lucid, the armenian wine merchant started rambling about his dreary circus years, he was ten when he joined the circus, the russian clowns raped him every day, and after they'd raped him they mimicked his shattered stagger, he drove me to his flat above a kitchen utensils shop, we wolfed down a port-soaked boar and a lamb-shaped iced cake and then i ripped off my clothes and straddled him, i jerked him off and put my clothes back on, i licked the remaining icing off my plate, "that makes me so nostalgic" he said, he took his plate and started spinning it on a stick, in no time it whirled so damn frantically i felt all giddy and a wee bit jealous cos i couldn't show him anything spectacular, quivering flesh is hardly spectacular, "teach me how to spin plates" i pleaded with him, after a few blowjobs and more quivering flesh he conceded, after 254 broken plates i finally got the knack of it, if only he could see me now, if only that wee fucking greedy self-obsessed cunt could come home, my skull is itching and i need a shot of spanish rum, don't give up, you've come this far you might as well go on, yes you're right, wee andy enters his kitchen, "don't just stare for fuck's sake, say something, drop your groceries and clap your hands if you're speechless", "those plates were my mother's", "is that all you can say? pffff, she would have clapped her hands", "no she wouldn't, she would have asked you to put them back in the cupboard next to the porcelain saucers", "i've spun the saucers too when you were out, i broke them all, i'm sorry", the wee gullible twat runs to his cupboard, i abruptly stop spinning the plates, they drop onto the floor, he turns around and comes over to me, "hit me if you want, but bear in mind that i have five sticks and fists that have to punch stout flemish fishmongers every bleeding night", and then he leaves again cos he forgot to buy flour, i glue the plates together again and start spinning, but it's just not the same now that i know that wee andy doesn't dig my act, i drop the plates, i stuff the broken plates in my handbag and pockets, i sit myself at the kitchen table and try to write a slanderous story about my sheffielder angel, i'm too hungover to properly slander him, i go into the living room and turn the television on, the empire strikes back, yoda is speaking german, i turn it off, wee andy enters, "are subtitles really expensive? yoda's not german, is he?", "of course not", "it was an armenian wine merchant who taught me how to spin plates", "that's great" he says all distractedly, "we ate lamb-shaped cake, he decapitated the lamb, strawberry syrup spurted on my white blouse, he used to spin plates for a russian circus, he called it 'drudgery', they also raped him every day, them russian clowns, they were really malicious bastards, i'm glad i never joined that circus", wee andy turns the television back on, jaws is speaking german, not jaws, but the tourists who are frivolously ignorantly swimming towards the beast, i wish someone would teach me how to dive more gracefully off the highest diving platform of that perv-infested north french swimming pool where the illiterate rentboy and i dive so clumsily every wednesday afternoon.

I AM TOO FREE FOR YOU / i'm sitting on a bench in the zoo, in front of the gloomy solitary sea cow who has greenish warts on his flank, the illiterate rentboy is sitting next to me, he wants to leave the zoo, he wants to get drunk in a seedy coastal pub and chat up some perverted australian priest, but i tell him: "not before you've made a beautiful drawing of a gloomy solitary mammal will we leave the zoo, get drunk in a seedy coastal pub and chat up some alcoholic perverted big-nosed australian priest", christopher gets up and sits himself in front of the restless siberian tiger, despite all the sedatives he still manages a fairly ferocious howl when i poke it in the groin with a wooden spike, "what did you do that for??", "it didn't look injured enough, it does now, shut your gob and draw the miserable beast", i enter the cafeteria and sit myself by the window from where i can see a wee monkey with a white head and a black body shudder on the upper branch of a sycamore, it's shuddering cos obnoxious and obese school kids are throwing empty cans and pebbles at it, stella from a plastic cup tastes odd, on my tray are three plastic cups of stella, three apples and a peanut butter sandwich; a flemish perv comes sitting opposite me, he tells me that his name is bert vander-cuntsomething and that he's tied up and gagged his two sons and laid their puny bodies in the ant bear's cave, i tell him that my name's delphine and that i've neither sympathy nor hand-jobs for a father who's just fed his spawn to a large edentate mammal of tropical america that feeds wholly or chiefly on ants, that's what it says in my brochure, i tell him that i feel a bit like the wee monkey up there, i point at the wee monkey with the white head who's violently shuddering and shrieking and still being harassed by ugly fat bored unimaginative over-privileged middle class kids, the flemish perv glances at the wee monkey and takes my wee chapped milk bottle stacker hands in his big manicured nefarious pimp hands, i pull my-self free from his grip and down my three cups of stella, on his tray are a cup of black coffee and two oranges, the oranges smell of gasoline, the flemish perv tells me that i need to "chill like that llama over there", but that llama over there is sedated, i know cos i overheard its malicious keepers, they were talk-ing about putting an extra dose of xanax in the llama's dinner cos it's been behaving so exuberantly lately and yesterday it spat at the mayor and took a bite out of some flemish painter's nose; i'm munching on an apple and assessing the flemish perv, his wallet and crotch are bulging so i decide to waste this dreary tuesday afternoon with him, but first i have to see christopher's drawing, there is no drawing!! the foolish rentboy is flirting with a chubby canadian tourist, the siberian tiger is hissing at me, i spit in its eye and throw russian abuse at it, it whimpers and hides in one of the corners of its piss-soaked cage, i introduce christopher to the flemish perv: "christopher, this is the flemish perv we're gonna give head to this afternoon", and then i introduce bert to the illiterate rent-boy: "bert, this is the illiterate rentboy you're gonna fuck and beat on the head with a flemish stove-pipe and pay good money to this afternoon"; we leave the zoo, bert is driving us to his place, christopher and i are sitting in the back seat, we're playing paper scissors stone; the perv's place is a wee apartment above an antiques shop, christopher and i sit ourselves in front of his flemish stove and press our cheeks against it, the perv comes back from the kitchen with a white tray that has a crack in the middle and red tulips in the corners, on the tray are three glasses of red wine and a whole assortment of stale biscuits, the illiterate rentboy wolfs them all down and then uses the perv's bathroom to vomit them all out, how do i know this for sure? i know this for sure cos there are gurgling, gagging, retching, and finally puking sounds coming out of the bathroom that's only a thin wall away, after christopher's bulimic antics we all get undressed, the flemish perv fondles and slaps our genitals for a few hours whilst christopher and i are wondering what it would be like to live in an ant bear's cave, maybe the ant bear would adopt us? maybe it'd rape us? maybe it'd suck us up with its long vacuum cleaner nozzle-like snout? it would definitely be a lot quieter in the ant bear's cave than in the ghastly bedsit we have to share with all those cancerous crack-crazed cats and manipulative hysterical dykes and gun-swaying deprived anorexic junkies and all their scary slavonic dealers and pimps, not to mention the minging russian hobos and spiteful armenian winos who are squatting and not getting along in the barren pantry; when the flemish perv's done with our genitals we walk back to the zoo and show the lady in the glass box the stamp on our hands, but it's faded so much, the myopic cunt claims we haven't got one and we have to pay again and receive a fresh stamp of a suicidal arctic fox on our hands, the ink smells of raspberry chewing gum and liquorice, we down a bottle of rum in the nocturama and wonder what it would be like to live above an antiques shop and be non-descript and unemployed, we shudder at the mere thought, we stagger out of the nocturama and smoke a few fags in front of the gloomy solitary sea cow, it looks as if it hasn't moved all day.

I WANT MORE THAN A QUICK PEEP / my sheffielder angel's bathtub is filled with dead freshwater fish and baby sharks, some are still twitching and flapping, i let the tap run to give them some oxygen, but the bath's too full and the fish drop on the floor and pretty soon the bathroom as well as the bedroom and corridor are littered with expensive suffering freshwater fish and baby sharks that are apathetically snapping at my calves, my sheffielder angel enters his apartment, he picks up the fish and stuffs them in his fridge and oven, he throws the baby sharks in his wardrobe and then he slaps me till my eyebrows start bleeding, he arsefucks me till i stop sniggering, i suck his cock and tell my sheffielder angel that i couldn't watch those freshwater fish so desperately writhe and choke on this dry smug air and not do anything about it, especially since they were suffering for a middle class orgy that i'm not invited to, my sheffielder angel slaps me till my eyelids burst open and my eardrums pop, he fingers me till i cry out in russian for the blind hobo who licked my minge so tenderly last night, i push him off me, spit in his chubby spoilt face and get dressed, i check on the fish in the fridge, but they're all dead, i snatch a heavy silver carp and run out of the apartment, i'm walking to wee andy's place, in the piss-soaked alley where i was once raped by a gang of rabies-crazed rumanian heroin pushers i bump into the dour german hobo who tried to shove his callous fist up my arse last tuesday, but i pulled out my stanley knife and sliced up his left eyeball, and that's why he's wearing a black patch over his left eye, i ask him if i can have a peep under his patch, "if i can have a peep under your skirt first" he says, "sure you can have a peep, but i have to warn you: my minge doesn't look very appetising today", the german hobo shrugs and lifts up my skirt, he pulls down my knickers and starts licking my cunt, i knee him in his healthy eye and remove the patch, i poke my finger in the slimy void, wipe it off on my skirt and run out of the alley, i take the bus to wee andy's place, a flemish perv comes sitting next to me: "why are you clutching a cuban grouper?", "it's not a cuban grouper, ignorant cunt, it's a danish silver carp, and i don't know why i'm clutching it, here, you can have it", i give the perv the danish silver carp and get off the bus, i'm standing in front of the library, i take the glass elevator to the flemish war poetry floor, borrow a dreadful anthology and suck the librarian's cock in a musty pantry that's filled with worm-infested novels and russian papers, the librarian's old and stingy and cynical, but he gives me dodgy scottish crime novels and flemish cookery books if i suck his cock passionately enough; after the blowjob the librarian gives me two german books on russian prostitution and two winston churchill biographies, i leave the library and finally make it to wee andy's snug street, i knock on his door, there's no one home, wee andy's neighbour opens his door and calls me inside, wee andy's neighbour is almost as sleazy and perverted as mine, but he pours more generous shots of german cognac and his right wing opinions are more moderate, i go inside and give him the churchill biographies, he pours me a stingy shot of calvados and offers me some austrian crack which i decline; i straddle wee andy's neighbour, unzip his pants, lift up his paunch and suck his limp middle-aged cock, after three hours it finally oozes a ghastly greenish liquid, i catch it in my palms and stare at it intently until the old cunt yanks my arm and rips off my blouse, "i have to go" i tell him, "i have to fondle your tits first" he says, "ok then", wee andy's neighbour fondles my tits until they're sore and bleeding, i put my blouse and skirt back on and take the two german books on russian prostitution with me, i leave the house and knock on wee andy's door, there's no one home, i sit myself on the doorstep and try to make sense of the german introduction.

IT'S HARD TO ENJOY RAPE SOMETIMES / "we are all very worried about you", that's what the kinky nightnurse says whilst unzipping my jeans, he says "we" but he means "i", he says "worried" but he means "eager to get into your knickers", i'm just glad i'm no longer trapped in that nuthouse, you can only get raped by a kinky nightnurse so many times before you lose your mind and end up stuck and subjected to his sleaze and sedatives for the rest of your life, like all those gorgeous anorexic orphan boys who'll be minging and bitter tomorrow; i'm still stuck and subjected to his sleaze and sedatives, but at least we're not in a white room, we're in the wee forest next to the disused factory where they make soap from the fat of whales and seals, or in the shape of whales and seals, or both, i can't remember; i was just minding my own business, i was reading a smug russian novel that i borrowed from wee andy months ago, the copulating pigeons were making it hard to concentrate though, and now i haven't even got a smug russian novel anymore, the kinky nightnurse threw it away and the sound of the flying novel wasn't the sound of copulating pigeons at all, or of any other copulating birds for that matter, just the sad lonely sound of rustling pages, they did sound a bit like dead leaves that are being walked on by labradors and their perverted owners; the kinky nightnurse hates nutters who read, he thinks russian novels are gonna give us the strength to run away from him, as if russian novels have that kind of power, wee andy will be devastated if he finds out that his russian novel was destroyed by a perv, it's beyond repair, it's lying in a puddle of mud and moss and dead leaves, some of the pages are stuck in nearby shrubs, one of the pages is stuck to the kinky nightnurse's raincoat, but he hasn't noticed yet, that's why i'm sniggering, he probably thinks i'm sniggering cos he's touching my cunt, but if it wasn't for that chapter stuck to his mac i'd be crying my heart out cos there's nothing sadder than being fondled by a cunt in a white coat, even if he isn't wearing a white coat right now, i'm not wearing my smudged apron, but that doesn't mean that i'm not a milk bottle stacker at this very moment, i'm wearing blue jeans and an oasis t-shirt and am being stroked by a sturdy kinky nightnurse who hates my guts but worships my genitals, i've got milk bottle stacker written all over my soul, there's no clocking off, but i guess it's different for nurses; he fucks me against a rain-soaked oak tree, i try to concentrate on the bark that's rubbing my back rather than on the cock that's brutalising my bowels, but it's hard; there's a red squirrel hopping in the upper branches of the oak tree, no actually i've been staring in the sun for too long, my sight's damaged beyond repair, it's hopping squirrels for me from now on, probably for the rest of my wretched life, but then the squirrel's gone; the kinky nightnurse is stark naked, i'm sucking his treacherous boner, he doesn't look vulnerable when he's stark naked, that's cos he's evil and his weapon is a forty inch boner, his spunk is poisonous, last time i swallowed it i almost lost my mind, i slept in a sheffielder gutter for a week, i dreamt about dostoyevsky and i was attacked by malicious aboriginals who wanted to skin me, that all sounds like a load of rubbish in retrospect, but it was pretty scary at the time; i swallow his cum nevertheless, i instantly start feeling terribly itchy and paranoid, i'm too scared to put my clothes back on, they might strangle me you know, so i run out of the wee forest stark naked, just praying i don't look too vulnerable, not really praying though, just pleading with the oak trees, i guess that's even worse; there are a few pages of wee andy's russian novel lying on the pavement, the wind sends them flying and i collide with them, i run to wee andy wrapped up in many many pages, but the wind's less ferocious here and it's drizzling and soon enough i'm stark naked again; there's a blanket lying on one of wee andy's horses, i cautiously approach the hostile beast but when i try to grab the blanket, the beast bites my throat, at least the blood makes me look less naked; i knock on wee andy's window, he's quite shocked when he sees me standing on his doorstep with a gaping throat and blood-soaked feet, he calls an ambulance and covers my body with a blanket that never covered any horse.

HE HAS NO MONGOLIAN RUG,BUT HE HAS A MUTE DONKEY AND A BLIND DALMATIAN / the flemish perv has finally fallen asleep, he chatted me up this morning at the library, i was leafing through a slanderous book about mongolian rugs and cutlery when all of a sudden this flemish geezer grabbed my arm, squeezed it and said: "i have a mongolian rug at my place, you can come and admire it if you want", i said: "that's really generous of you, i would love to admire it, can i take a picture of it?", "sure" he said, "take as many pictures as you want, honey" he added, so he drove me to his place, i moaned a lot in his car, mostly about my sheffielder angel's reluctant testicles, and also about the illiterate rentboy's obnoxious cheerfulness, a boy who gets fucked up the arse and maimed with rusty candelabra by middle-aged clerics every minute of every night shouldn't be that cheerful, he should be miserable and losing his hair, but instead he's whistling daft britpop songs and combing his fringe for hours on end, bless him, and i moaned about wee andy, the fickle bitch is angry with me cos i gave his wheelbarrow to an unfortunate north french peasant, he can be so callous, it's not like he even used it, it was just standing in his shed, there was a dormouse sleeping in it, i chased it away, it broke my heart but the peasant needed the wheelbarrow more, i walked all the way to the french countryside with that bloody rusty creaking wheelbarrow, the peasant was hardly grateful: "you said that it was in mint condition?!" was what he said, "fuck you, you fucking ungrateful rural twat" i said and kicked the wheelbarrow into a nearby swamp, it sank, i felt sorry then, mostly for myself, what a waste of time, i fucked the peasant, i had to do something to make the trip seem like less of a waste of time, it was a mediocre shag, i walked back to belgium on my knees as a penance for having wasted all that time, but after ten minutes i got bored of doing penance, i kicked off my shoes and ran to the nearest petrol station, i got a lift from a thick flemish plumber, he stopped the car in the car park of a closed sea life centre, he fondled my tits for a while, i asked him if i could touch his toolbox, it was a metaphor, but he got out of the car, opened his trunk and put his toolbox on my lap, i opened it, i said: "you can maim my minge with this funky screwdriver if you want", "i'm not into that kind of stuff" he said, he ripped off my jeans and slapped my minge for two hours, and then he drove me to wee andy's place, i told wee andy everything, it was very painful, i stuck to the truth cos i was so fed up with lying, and it was a brutal and exciting truth anyway, but all that wee stingy cunt said was: "you stole my wheelbarrow", over and over again until i knocked him unconscious with his bass guitar, i put compresses on his eyes and left the house; when i entered the flemish perv's house i was shuddering with anticipation, so happy i was that i'd finally get to see a real authentic mongolian rug, but there was no mongolian rug, there was awkward sex on a curry-stained shag carpet for eight hours on end, the flemish perv bragged a lot during the sex, about all the money he gives to charity, about all the colombian rentboys he taught how to spell and shoot, about all the sultry french vixens he's wooed and corrupted and about all the siberian tigers he's tamed and taught how to drive burning police cars wearing silly hats and cardigans, but then one day a poodle bit his ankle, and now he's on sick-leave, i blow a lash off his cheek and call wee andy: "andy, it's me", "hmm, what do you want?", "your forgiveness and your groin", "i can give you the former", "WELL THAT'S AWFULLY GENEROUS", i hang up on that stingy cunt and wake up the flemish perv cos i'm aching to fuck and to hear more about those colombian rentboys he taught how to gracefully jump off burning pyramids wearing pink jockstraps and black eyeliner, he yawns, stretches himself, enters me and starts rambling about his literary ambitions, "I DON'T WANT TO HEAR

ABOUT YOUR ABORTED NOVELS, I WANT TO HEAR ABOUT THE CIRCUS" i snap, he punches me in the face and continues moaning about his dour unimaginative fucking unfaithful muse.

I'M THE CRIPPLE ONE THEN,IS THAT IT ?! / "fucking ghastly", wee andy is asking me what i think of his paintings, "atrocious, sterile, ugly, depressing, boring, shallow, pretentious, fucking middle class, no mate, i don't like them, i think you should stick to spreadsheets and sucking corporate cock", "that's a bit harsh", "i'm only being honest", "i only spent three years of my life painting these", "three years in which you could have been beating up poofs, sniffing glue, mugging old tarts, saving wounded pigeons, eating glass, wanking with toggled hand harpoons, shagging illiterate ex-rentboys, torturing nocturnal rodents, burning down libraries, arsefucking welsh sheep and whatnot, but no, you had to waste all those years making fuckawful paintings and thinking up pedantic titles, as if the world hasn't got enough fuckawful paintings with pedantic titles as it is", wee andy's looking at me as if i just scratched his new flash car, which incidentally i did, he just doesn't know yet; i look again at the paintings: i study them a bit closer, still fucking ghastly, i take my black marker and write a few stories on them: that's better, "you fucking cunt, you ruined them!", "tsk tsk tsk, i improved them", i've never seen the wee middle class cunt so fucking angry, i didn't think he had it in him, what with all his hippy bollocks about patience and forgiveness, but right the now i think he's about to kick my head in, and he hasn't even seen his car yet, or his trashed living room for that matter, not to mention his decapitated golden retrievers, i'm not gonna hang around till he finds out, i've wasted enough time here already, i don't even know why i came here in the first place, to bait the wee middle class twat i suppose, boredom, no fucking inspiration, not a cock in sight, how many reasons do you need? i jump out of wee andy's bedroom window and i run to the nearest pub, which is not near cos the wee overprivileged middle class cunt lives in a posh smug safe fucking sterile suburb far away from all the seedy pubs and their seedy spawn, far away from anything remotely exciting; the pub is crowded, there's a one-legged perv standing at the bar, i've never shagged a one-legged perv before so i go over to the geezer and start chatting him up, which should be easy enough, cos not many girls chat up cripple pervs three times their age: "how are things?", "things are fine, can i buy you a drink?", "by all means, buy away, let's get pissed and shag each other's brains out", "erm", "stella will be fine", "there you go", "tell me, do you play any instruments?", "i actually play three instruments: the piano, the violin and the tuba", "you must be pulling my leg", "no, i'm serious, i'm a musician", "i'm a writer", "i'm sure you are, love", "don't fucking patronise me, crippled cunt", "are you always this nasty?", "i'm being nicer than usual, cos you're cripple", "piss off", "don't be so fucking oversensitive, you should be grateful that you're being chatted up by a two-legged girl who could well be your granddaughter", "actually i'm married and my wife's got a nice pair of legs", well that's me gutted, first i'm being subjected to wee andy's fuckawful paintings and now i'm being rejected by a one-legged perv, could this day get any worse? of course it can: the spiteful busker is standing at a deserted bus stop mumbling some shit about a minging slag who blackens his name: "daddy, so good to see you, read my new story please, it's right up your alley, it's about nocturnal rodents that are being shoved up the arses of rotten twisted adults, mostly politicians and priests", i hand the vicious cunt my new story but he just tears it up, "but you haven't even read it!!?!", "i don't have to read it to know that it's rubbish", "oh, ok, what do you think of my new sweater? i bought it in dublin", "fucking ghastly", "dublin?", "your sweater", "oh, ok, well come on, give us another one of your incest ballads!!" but instead of placating his audience, the spiteful cunt trashes his guitar on my back, rips my sweater to shreds and steals my wallet.

I HOPE YOU CHOKE ON THAT SELF-PITY,MISERABLE CUNT / my bedsit is full of flies and they're dying, every hour their movements become a little slower and they no longer fly away when i raise my hand like i'm about to crush them, you are a pathetic cunt i yell at the fattest fly, when i'm really talking to myself, for all i know the flies might be thinking the exact same about me, that i'm slowly dying, but i'm not, i still fight and fuck, though more often the latter; the only thing i'm good at is stealing fat wallets from conceited yuppie scum, or from poor old defenceless ladies for that matter, but money is the only thing i don't need, and i usually end up giving it to christopher who squanders it at the fair and comes home with giant fuckawful orange teddy bears that don't even fit in what has now become his bedsit rather than mine, sometimes he comes home with a depressed goldfish but it always dies before we've even given it a name; the shower tray is still mine, it's where i go when i need to bleed, when i need to cut the caked spunk out of all my orifices, and it's where i write my crap stories that haven't even got a narrative and that seem to alienate all my middle class friends, which is just as well, cos i don't want middle class friends in my life, they're cruel in a polite way, i'd rather have people around me that are cruel in a blatant way cos i'm confused enough as it is; sure i miss wee andy, but since he won't rape me nor save me, he's pretty much useless to me; i don't know how the rentboy manages to be so fucking cheerful about being brutally arsefucked by rotten twisted adults every bleeding day, i don't know how he manages to sleep but it pisses me off, so i wake him up, but i've forgotten what it is that i wanted to say, there's nothing i want to say to the illiterate cunt, i just want him to be just as alert as me, he shouldn't sleep in a world that's inhabited by nefarious pimps and incestuous swine who are out to get us, but being scared is like dying or coming, you have to go through it alone, and christopher just wants to sleep and we can talk about it tomorrow, but tomorrow is so far away and i feel extremely sad like i just lost my job at the supermarket and am now officially an outlaw, but i'm not, cos tomorrow i'll be stacking milk bottles and cursing those relentless neon lights, and rudiger my gregarious german colleague will be there and i'll cut myself and he'll bandage my wounds and ask me why i cut myself and i won't tell but i'll feel all warm and mellow cos he asked, and he always asks, but not in a dodgy comforting-whilst-undoing-my-bra way, in a fatherly way, a real father not an incestuous swine; i'm going over to my dodgy neighbour, cos i'm too tired to walk to some deserted church or seedy pub and be chatted up by russian cow killers or french porn stars, i don't really care if his body's old and his cock's limp and smelly, i just want to be hugged and hit and forget all about my psycho grandfather who's still haunting me and will be haunting me for the rest of my life cos the cunt died so peacefully, i wanted him to die at my feet, by my hand, writhing and choking and looking helpless and scared forever; or maybe i just want to get pissed and come under a headless cuckoo clock, my dodgy neighbour says that i'm making an old man very happy, which makes me some kind of saint then, i feel really repulsive though like i'm the one with the old saggy flesh and grey pubes, i feel big and awkward, and i wish the cunt would stop telling me how beautiful i am, i'm not, i'm minging, and i'm not sweet, i'm spiteful, but he can't see it cos he's looking at my genitals, and my genitals are as eager as ever, throbbing away, and the headless cuckoo comes out and despite being headless it cuckoos four times which means i have to get ready for work; the supermarket is looking homely, i put on my baggy dark blue sweater with the supermarket logo on the back, and my smudged apron and my name tag that says "zoë smekens" which is my milk bottle stacker name, i clock in, i cut myself with my stanley knife, but instead of rudiger an old dour big-nosed flemish cunt bandages my wounds, loveless and distractedly, he calls me an attention-seeking cunt, but i don't want just any attention, i want rudiger's.

I'M PUTTING THE LID ON THE NIGHT / i wasn't coming, i was choking, i was chewing a plastic smurf but i accidentally inhaled it, i had to sit up and puke it out, but he was holding me down whilst eating my cunt, his hands were pressing my arms against the wooden floor, when i tried to breathe i got no air, only this terrible pain in my chest until i couldn't struggle any longer, i saw myself lying there in the piss-soaked corridor, stark naked, bluish, i was wheezing and then i passed out; the cunt who took my death throes for an orgasm was the spanish stud who lives downstairs with his fiery feral wife and very blond wee daughter; anyway i don't know who saved me, maybe i'm not saved at all cos there's still a lump down my throat and every time i swallow i want to run away, but i can't run away from this, the wee smurf will always be stuck down my throat, or further down in my lungs, at least i can breathe now; christopher is sleeping with his right hand cupped around his balls, his other hand is clinging to a stuffed seal's nylon whiskers; i call my sheffielder angel, but his answer to my distress, anxiety, and panic is "take care of a wee animal, save the third world, write a beautiful story about meadows and sheep, go see a shrink, wank yourself to sleep", when really he should be saying: kill the cunt that spawned you, carve my name into your groin with a pair of scissors, come over to sheffield and stalk me, go back to the old hooking game, steal, hurt, maim, plagiarise, destroy, obliterate etc etc, so i slam down the phone and i sit on the window sill and nothing's reassuring, lots of stars but no constellations, there's an r.e.m. song coming from the house right across ours, it's about andy kaufmann, i wanted to be andy kaufmann when i was a child, and after that i wanted to be michael stipe cos i thought he was so very sensual, that only lasted a few months, and now i'm perfectly ok with being a minging orphan girl, and the fact that there's no respect nor success out there for sluts like us does make me angry at times, but there's not much that i can do about it, and at least i'm not illiterate and thick and fat like my sweet rent-boy sidekick; there's a dog collar, cutlery and letters strewn across the pavement, the letters are addressed to me, not quite love letters, not quite death threats, blackmail i suppose you could call it, they're all from the retarded flemish cook, he expects a little tenderness in return for all that money and jewelry i didn't ask for but squandered and pawned all the same, i can't give him tenderness cos i loathe him, i can give him my cunt and tits, and sometimes selling those in exchange for tacky tinsel brooches and a measly tenner doesn't seem like a fair bargain, other times when i'm less gloomy it just seems too fucking easy to just lie there stark naked, wide open, cold, motionless and hostile, ripping off all those wretched johns; i'm adding a few scars to my pale puny body, i'm using the lid of an asparagus jar, i stole the asparagus jar cos it reminded me of that ghastly flemish singer/songwriter i once fancied for a day, i'm sentimental like that, i'm carving his name into my arm, but i slip and his name's unreadable, which is just as well cos it's a long ugly guttural name and i don't wanna be reminded of him every time i write, wank, fuck, fight or whatever; i'm losing blood and it's dripping onto the love letters, this would all be very romantic if my wounds weren't self-inflicted and if the letters weren't coming from a retarded flemish cook who has no chin and lives with his mother; i can hear my dodgy neighbour's headless cuckoo clock when i press my ear against the wall which i am doing now, it's three am, the sleazy cunt is arsefucking someone who sounds underage, boyish and scared; i call up wee andy: "please hold the line.......hi, this is andrew, i'm afraid i'm not around but...", how fucking rude, i bet he's sleeping, how dare he sleep whilst i'm bleeding on my window-sill?!! i bandage my arms and get ready for work, christopher is holding a scruffy stuffed panda bear in his arms, it's scruffy cos it's been tied gagged raped beaten whipped slandered locked humiliated denied and whatnot for seventeen years, i don't know who gave it to me, i gave it to the rentboy but i didn't tell him where and with whom it had been and what they had done to it, i told him i won it at the fair.

I CAN HEAR YOUR HEARTBEAT IN MY MINGE / i've promised christopher i'd try to write a "sweet innocent story", i am sitting at my dodgy neighbour's kitchen table, i'm stark naked but i feel very warmly dressed, it's because i'm covered with four layers of spunk and wax, my neighbour's pouring water on flemish flour, he's making bread, it's ludicrous when psychopaths do homely stuff, i'm trying to write a sweet innocent story, this is what i've got so far: "the sea is very restless tonight. wee ian is reading a scottish novel about chivalrous carpenters and malicious english warmongers. he can't concentrate though, he's thinking of his french girlfriend. a flemish perv offers wee ian a cigarette." my dodgy neighbour pours me a pint of rum, i scowl at it, "down it or you're a dead cat", i down it, he rubs his limp scabby cock against my elbow, i ignore it, "suck it or you're a dead cat", i suck it, i spit his cum in my empty pint and resume writing: "wee ian eagerly accepts the fag and shows the perv the book he's reading. the perv scoffs at the hideous cover. there are fireworks in the north french sky. wee ian loves fireworks." my dodgy neighbour is kneading dough and whistling a cliff richard song, he throws a slab of dough in front of me, i spit at it, "knead it or you're a dead cat", i pick the slab up and drop it behind his flemish stove, "retrieve it or you're a dead cat!" he yells, but i just roll my eyes and leave the kitchen, i lie myself under his cuckoo clock and shoot that miserable austrian bird with my imaginary rifle, i punch myself in the face with the barrel of my imaginary rifle and close my eyes, i can hear the old cunt climbing the stairs to his attic, he's fetching rope and garden tools, every thursday he ties me up, maims my back with a garden rake and teaches me how to conjugate irregular flemish verbs, that's why my flemish is so poor, my back and wrists always hurt too much to concentrate, my dodgy neighbour drags me from under the cuckoo clock and ties my feet together, he ties my hands to the ugliest leg of his german table, the one that's cracked and blood-specked, they're all cracked and blood-specked, but this one just sticks out, he punches me in the nape: "you scream and you're a dead cat", "YEAH YEAH YEAH, i should have been a dead cat when i refused to knead your dough, and then when i dropped that slab behind your stove and didn't retrieve it, i should have been a dead cat then too, old useless crippled racist retarded minging alcoholic incestuous flemish twat", "a cat has nine lives" he says and stabs his rake in my back, i cry out in pain, "six lives left" he wheezes, "oh shut up, you old spiteful unimaginative mediocre spineless dour sadistic narrow-minded boorish boisterous sim...", my dodgy neighbour gags me with a swiss table cloth, he shoves a sandy shovel up my arse, gleefully twists it, pulls it out, ungags me, "don't stare at me when i'm fondling your tits, dead cat", i glare at an atrocious still life of two flemish apples and a gloomy stuffed pheasant instead, my neighbour unties my feet, and then my hands, i spit in his face, fend off his punches and stagger to the kitchen, he pours brownish disinfectant on my back, i pick up my pencil: "the flemish perv starts rubbing wee ian's frail boyish crotch. wee ian is upset but also aroused. the fireworks are gorgeous, he comes, he pretends he's yelping ecstatically because of the fireworks. the flemish perv chuckles. the flemish perv knows how self-conscious frigid middle class twats get after their cums. how harsh and fucking unfaithful they behave afterwards. so fucking harsh and so fucking unfaithful it's best to bludgeon them to death, to bury them in the dunes and to forget all about them." i put on my dodgy neighbour's dark blue sweater and stuff my face with sour soppy waffles, we share a bottle of bourbon, i bite his thin lower lip and tenderly caress his soft groin, "stop biting or you're a dead kitten", he's changed it to "kitten", how cute, i bite my thumb and rub his tacky tinsel rings, i straddle him, i can feel the wounds on my back burst and throb, i don't care, i want a cum, i take his apathetic index finger, lead it to my minge and show it about, when i come i think of wee andy.

three

MY MOTHER'S MINGE IS LIKE A TURKISH AMBUSH / my dodgy neighbour is feeding me french fries and undercooked reindeer loins, it's scary to eat with tied hands, but when i press my lips together he pokes me in the eye with his fork and threatens to shove a knife up my nose, i don't know why he's so eager to stuff me with food, most pervs prefer me anorexic, he unties my hands and puts a pint of rum in front of me, i down it and ask him if i can dust and polish his flemish crossbows in the garage, he drags me down the stairs and into the garage and shows me which cloth and which brand of beeswax i'm supposed to use for each of the crossbows, it's all very confusing, there are two hundred cloths, twenty jars of beeswax and a thousand crossbows, my dodgy neighbour leaves the garage and locks and bolts all the exits, i dust a bottle of bourbon and take a few swigs, i stroke a few arrows and throw two in the air and try to gracefully catch them, one falls on the floor and the other pierces my right foot, i cry out in pain, my dodgy neighbour enters the garage, i point at my foot in horror, but he just rolls his eyes and leaves again, "DON'T PANIC, YOU FUCKING USE-LESS OVERSENSITIVE TART!" i shout and punch myself in the nose, more blood, i think i'm gonna pass out, i scratch the walls for help, i'm just being theatrical, i hop on my dodgy neighbour's work table, i tear up all his designs for flemish escutcheons and sit myself in a musty wicker chair, i tap the floor with the beeswax jar, i tap a nice frantic rhythm, i drum the table with two arrows, my dodgy neighbour enters the garage, he smashes the rim of the jar with a hammer and drags me upstairs, he pours disinfectant on my foot and bandages it clumsily and angrily, he lifts me and puts me on his austere german table, "dance for me", i sway my hips apathetically, "your dancing sucks", "i know, maybe i could recite a poem instead?", "NO", "it's about my mother's minge", "go on then", i put my hands behind my back and cough solemnly: "my mother's minge is like a seedy tattoo parlour that's owned by a hirsute norwegian contract killer/ it looks dangerous and exciting, but if you value your life more than a cum don't fill her/ my mother's minge is like a dodgy yankee remake of a hitchcock flick/ the teeth are whiter, but the plot's as irksome as the cattle tick/ my mother's minge is like a cancerous poodle that's whimpering in the handbag of a conceited tart/ you want to bludgeon it to death, but not to ferociously fondle and kiss it first is hard/ my mother's minge is like a lice-infested welsh sheep in the middle of the road/ you want to run it over, but first you want to rock the boat/ my mother's minge is like a rabies-crazed squirrel that snubs your nuts/ you want to stuff it and squeeze it, even though you hate her guts/ my mother's minge is like a turd on an immaculate street/ you don't tread, but you fall on your knees and knead/ my mother's minge is like a silvery shrub in a bleak french reservoir/ it looks so biblical, but it will only drive you to the next coastal bar/ my mother's minge is like a drunk stand-up comedian on your last train home/ it's hardly laughable, but at least you're not alone", "disappointing ending" my neighbour says gruffly and ungratefully, he drags me off his table, rips off my skirt, pulls down my knickers and shoves his long athletic tongue in my cunt, he stirs and slides and slaps and tickles, i come for many many minutes, maybe for half an hour, i forget the glass splinters in my sole, i forget the unflinching churlish dour corporate manners of my sheffielder angel, i forget how disarmingly wee andy blushes when i show him the scars on the inside of my thighs, i forget to worry about the illiterate rentboy, my dodgy neighbour punches me in the face, my minge stops tingling, my foot starts to ache and swell again, i take a swig from his bottle of german cognac, i pour some on my foot and hop outside, the coastal night is ugly and balmy, i sit myself on my doorstep and press an empty beer can against my foot, a minging russian hobo passes, i tug at his sleeve, scrounge a fag, light it, have a deep wholesome drag, and ask the hobo if he wants a story or a funny dance in return, he wants the funny dance.

I AM WITHOUT RESTRAINT,DESPITE MY RESTRAINING ORDER / i have to talk to wee andy, no restraining order's gonna stop me, the people at my wretched building are driving me mad, i'm so sick of being blackmailed, then don't give them the chance to blackmail you, that's what wee andy would say, the moralist twat, but it's not that simple; i can't move out either, it's too late for that, i'm gonna die between festering rodents, whimpering junkies, abusive drunkards and manipulative orphan girls, it's inevitable, just call me a fatalist, or a sad cunt if you're not too keen on big words; at least i don't have to pay rent anymore, the landlord's too frightened to come round and claim it, and the police are just waiting for the place to fall apart, but it's not gonna fall apart, deluded pigs ,we'll just continue baiting, mugging and stabbing each other til we die unnatural and untimely deaths, but we'll be replaced by other scum before you can say "uninhabitable"; still it was nice to have one sane middle class friend on whose smug middle class sofa i could crash out, just call me an opportunist, or a scrounger if you're not too keen on big words; i trashed wee andy's interior- and that is not some dirty metaphor- about a hundred times, i burnt down his house, i pissed on his ghastly oil paintings- improving them rather than ruining them, although he didn't see it that way-, i ripped all his poof clothes to shreds, i pawned his obscure indie albums, i paraded my scars, burns, cuts, bruises, big gaping wounds, despair, squalor, spite and slashed cunt into his face; i plagiarised his frankly embarrassing poems and won a few dodgy contests with them, i was even invited to swansea to collect my fuckawful trophy, i had to give a speech, in welsh; i tore up his father's suicide note; i made a bonfire of all his insipid pompous yankee novels, it was bliss watching all those neurotic lousy little writers catching fire, i particularly enjoyed watching philip roth go up in flames, the cunt had been bugging me for years, moaning like that about his poor old mother who bloody well paid for the cunt's education, first house, wedding and whatnot, fucking over-privileged middle class twat; but wee andy was always so sympathetic, so fucking forgiving, until, inevitably, he had to fall in love with a prissy stuck-up middle class slag who brainwashed him, she bloody well poisoned him with all her sad little middle class principles, restrictions more like; she told him that i'm no good for him and that he should stop seeing me, as if a frigid unimaginative middle class prude is so much better for him; what wee andy needs is a sex monster, an unpredictable self-destructive reckless orphan slag like myself; wee andy needs me, i'm not some obsessive stalker for fuck's sake; the wee cunt's reading some music magazine, or actually he's merely staring at the pictures, pictures of some skinny doe-eyed dreamy indie boy who's wearing a skimpy cardigan, i bet the closet poof's got a boner, i knock on the window, he jumps up from the sofa looking rather scared, i try to reassure him, "it's ok, i'm not here to assault you, i just need a chat, and a hug (and a shag and a drink and another shag and a few more drinks)", but he can't hear me and he's picking up his phone, he's forming a number, a short number, and now he seems to be engaged in some frantic conversation, a three digits number, i think that's my cue to get the hell out of here.

FEAR, FOG AND CRUISING WITH RUDIGER / "that sheffielder cunt can fuck right off", rudiger just sighs cos this is all i've been saying for days now and the supermarket has run out of disinfectant and bandages, the sheffielder cunt doesn't even know that i'm bleeding, i'm lying on the floor in the infirmary pretending to be devastated, when really i just needed an excuse to throw myself on the floor and slash my arms with my new stanley knife, and that sheffielder cunt's betrayal is as good an excuse as any, "that sheffielder cunt, that bloody boring middle class twat who couldn't write a decent story to save himself, he had the nerve to call my stories BLEAK", "lordy", "DON'T FUCKING PATRONISE ME", rudiger is sitting on his knees at my side pressing a damp cloth against my left arm, it feels cool and hot at the same time, and i'm tingling all over like i'm about to come and pass out: "rudiger i'm scared, what will become of me??", but rudiger just ignores me, he's bandaging my left arm, i wish he'd finger me, or at least caress my tits, i'm gagging for it, "i'm feeling randy", "what?", "i'm feeling dandy, please let me get back to work", "i'm gonna drive you to the hospital, you need stitches", "if it isn't a sheffielder hospital, you can fuck right off", "it isn't a sheffielder hospital", on our way to the hospital i try to sulk but i can't keep it up, i've just too much to say: "that sheffielder cunt can fuck right off, he slagged off my stories, AS IF I GIVE A FUCK, do you really think i'm that vain?! pfff, he can slag them off all he wants, but next time he invites me over to suck his wee boner, i'm gonna bite it off and sell it on ebay", "who would buy it though?", "that's not the point, smart cunt, the point is that i'm gonna bite off his cock, in fact i'm gonna bite off every cock i encounter from now on, those are a whole lot of cocks, the male population will be proper traumatised, they'll all turn gay, there will be no more babies from now on, no more threats, no more incest, no more cock-eyed writers, no more lousy milk bottle stackers, no more spiteful orphan girls, no more restraining orders and no more fucking unfaithful sheffielder middle class cunts", rudiger is shifting in his seat, i stare at his crotch just to bait him, of course i'm not gonna bite it off, i'd be sent to prison, and prison is ghastly, i know cos my father lived there for a while, that's why he's so spiteful and homophobic i suppose, or maybe he was born spiteful and homophobic, or maybe he turned spiteful and homophobic on the day i was cut from my mother's belly, anyway i'm trying to avoid prison cos there's not enough cock in prison, and there's too much time, and i can't think of many things i want to do with my time except for sucking cock; "turn that up!!", "what?", "the song, turn it up", it's a sad sad song about a sad sad boy who lives in a sad sad industrial town, his father is an incestuous swine and his mother is an alcoholic hag, the boy has only one friend, his cat, and the cat's called 'fog', and the boy drowns fog because he's afraid his mother might hurt the cat, "please turn that rubbish off, i can't take it anymore", we drive along deserted streets, it's still very early, those bloody seagulls are awake though, they're laughing at me cos i'm pathetic and wounded, "rudiger, i fear that i'm losing my mind, the houses are staring at my tits and the trees are telling me to throw myself of the cliffs and take you with me", "you're not losing your mind, that person from sheffield hurt you and...", "you mean that sheffielder cunt who cruelly rejected me after shamelessly having fawned on me for months??", "yes", "he can fuck right off", "so you keep saying", "rudiger, i fear that my heart has stopped beating", rudiger puts his hand on my chest, which i hoped for, "it's still beating", "rudiger, i fear i will be stacking milk bottles and sucking dodgy cock for the rest of my life, i fear that's my destiny, i also fear that i'm only mildly talented, and i so badly want to be a genius so i can tell that sheffielder cunt to fuck right off, i also fear that i'm quite unlovable and that my bottom's too big, i fear that i'll be eaten alive by my cats when i'm eighty and still writing incoherent bollocks, i've many fears, rudiger, i also fear that i will bleed to death if we keep driving around like this", "we're almost there", and true enough, there it is: the most ghastly hospital in the world, "i fear that i'm too weak to walk by myself", and yet again i throw myself on the ground and pretend to be dead, rudiger picks me up and carries me inside, the doctor is a dour flemish cunt who's obviously never sniffed glue or wanked over ian curtis pictures in his locker, he oozes boredom, bloody awful poetry and catholicism, i hate his guts, rudiger seems so small and sweet and harmless compared to that dour cunt, i think about the supermarket when the flemish cunt is stitching me up, how i long to embrace those milk bottles again, "how i dread to go back to the supermarket, rudiger", "ach, you'll be alright", "i fear that i will die if i hear all those crap eighties songs about unrequited love, i fear that i will throw myself on the floor and cut myself all over again, over and over and over and over until i die", "please don't be so morbid", "please don't be such a bore", on our way back to the supermarket i manage to sulk for five minutes, but the german cunt just ignores me: "rudiger, let's kill horses", "what? why? what horses?", "never fucking mind, unimaginative twat", my arms are bandaged from my shoulders to my wrists, i can't bend them, "rudiger, i can't bend my arms!! people will think i'm disabled, they'll point and laugh at me, how am i supposed to write like this, let alone wank?? please put me out of my misery, i'm not enjoying this life so much anymore", "stop moaning, the bandages are only temporary", i'm sulking again, but this time for real, there's a sad sad song on the radio about a sad sad dog who lives in a sad sad pound, then one day a mancunian thug adopts him, and then somehow the dog gets decapitated, but i'm not sure cos it's in german, and my german is not that good, despite my fondness for rudiger.

KITTENS IN THE BOILER / the girl who drags frozen heifers off butcher hooks, chops them and wraps them in plastic for a living, she's gorgeous; when i stand on my ladder stacking pineapple jam jars i can see her relentlessly chopping away, i love heifers, but i love the butcher girl more, and i'm standing in front of her now, the stench of blood and stainless steel is making me retch, it's hard to chat up a girl in these conditions, besides, she's ignoring me, she thinks i'm weird, but the butcher who's seen me naked many times and wants to see me naked more, he's thrilled to see me, he's holding a big red slab of meat in his arms, he's rocking it, maybe even lulling it, and he comes over to me and hugs me and i can feel the cold slab soak my sweater and i throw up on the cold blood-smeared floor, the butcher is driving me home whilst the butcher girl is cleaning up my puke; he's not driving me home of course, he's driving me to some place where he can do things to my naked body without being bothered by an obnoxious rentboy or a jealous flemish retard, he's still wearing his blood-smudged apron, it's ghastly, i ask him if he can take it off but he just chuckles, quite maliciously i should add; he puts on the radio and all the songs are about fucking, and one song is about poisoned rain, it's all rubbish, i ask him to turn it off but he just shrugs and unzips my jeans, he's fingering me and the landscape is getting bleaker, we're somewhere hostile and coastal, the few people on the streets have buck teeth, i know this cos they bare them as we pass by, i don't want to fuck the butcher cos butchers drag frozen heifers off hooks, chop them and wrap them in plastic for a living, and there's nothing arousing about that, when i was ten i promised myself i'd never fuck a butcher, not even if they were clean and smelled of jasmine and oranges, but two years ago i gave my first vicious russian cow killer a blowjob for a tenner, and after that i never really stopped fucking butchers; his place is ghastly, there's a boiler in the living room and every time someone in his building takes a shower or does the dishes it sounds like kittens are being tortured inside, but there are no kittens, just a wobbly boiler in a dreary flemish living room, just a repulsive butcher three times my age who insists on wearing his blood-smudged apron when we fuck, all the stuff in his pockets falls on the floor when he's banging me: a blood-stained stanley knife, his mobile phone, scraps of paper, orders for heifers to be executed, telephone numbers of other butchers; he whines when he cums, but it's nothing like the whine of a heifer that's about to be executed, it's much like too many other pervs i've heard whining as they came, as if they lose something when they spurt inside a minging orphan girl, i don't whine and i don't come; we're drinking cheap spanish beer, i'm still naked but i don't feel self-conscious; i just don't love him enough to feel awkward or ugly, there's a speck of blood on my left thigh, but it's not from one of the many dead heifers on his apron, it's my blood, my nose is bleeding, he punched me in the nose cos i was laughing at his old saggy testicles, i'm not laughing now, i'm drinking cheap spanish beer and thinking of ways to charm the gorgeous butcher girl, but i don't know of any ways; he goes into the kitchen and washes his hands, the kittens start moaning again and i put my hands to my ears cos it sounds so much like there are real kittens inside that boiler, and they're being tortured; we fuck again, this time he takes off his apron, this time he fucks me till i whine and cry for mercy, and when he's not giving me any, i cry for help, but the kittens are smothering my cries.

IT'S ALL ABOUT FINDING AN APPROPRIATE BIRTHDAY PRESENT FOR WEE ANDY / the flemish john has tacky crystal geese on his mantelpiece, they have pink beaks and indigo eyes, he's sitting on his couch stark naked, he's got bruises on his shins and a huge scar on his left thigh, he's got hair on his belly and a tanned hard-on, he chatted me up in the coastal tram, i was on my way to wee andy's house, he sat himself next to me and started rambling about his script, it was very difficult to follow cos it was science fiction and in dutch, "it sounds like an expensive film" i said, "don't be so vulgar, not everything's about money" he snapped, we got off at the closed russian orphanage and walked to his place, i straddle him, he rips off my blouse and bra and starts kneading my tits, "why are there crystal kittens on your television set?", "cos my wife put them there", "can i have one?", "no", it's wee andy's birthday tomorrow, i've not enough money to buy him golden stirrups, and i've not enough sentimentality to write him a cheesy poem, a crystal kitten would be just perfect, "can i have a glass of wine?", "sure", he goes to the cupboard next to the television set, "LEMONADE! i want a glass of lemonade", "we don't have any lemonade", "where do you keep your port?", "in the fridge", "where's the fridge?", "in the kitchen", "then i want port", he rolls his eyes and goes to the kitchen, science fiction, pffff, no one wants your dodgy script, pffff, and everything's about money, if it wasn't i wouldn't be here and i wouldn't have to stuff a crystal kitten in the inside pocket of my fake leather jacket, and i wouldn't be wearing fake leather, and you wouldn't be whistling a blur song in your immaculate kitchen, so piss off, mediocre self-important middle class twat, he walks back into the living room and gives me a pint of white port, i take a cautious swig, "i don't like this, it's too sweet, don't you have any beer?" he goes back to the kitchen, i put the kitten back on the television set, i just know i'll feel guilty for 742 hours if i steal it, the flemish john is back with a bottle of stella, "i never drink from the bottle, it's so unbecoming for a lady to drink from the bottle, even if the lady's a whore", he snorts and goes back to the kitchen, i snatch the kitten and stuff it in my handbag, i just know i'll feel guilty for at least 950 hours if i don't have an appropriate birthday present for that wee conceited over-privileged jock, i down the stella, the perv is back, he gives me the glass, "i spilled the beer on my jeans", he feels them, "they're not wet", "you were gone for a long time", "no i wasn't... never mind, i'll fetch you another one", he leaves again, i stuff another crystal kitten in my handbag and take off my jeans, the flemish john gives me the stella, i take a swig, he pushes me down onto the couch and pulls down my knickers, two is such an awkward number, two is not a charm, two is just plain ugly, like copulating flies on a handmade austrian table cloth, i'll have to steal one more, there are eight left, seven is a solid number, besides, he seems like the kind of short-tempered alcoholic bastard who'll trash her crystal kittens when she's eight months pregnant and refuses to suck his precious boner, he enters me, maybe i should steal the geese instead of the kittens, maybe i should steal their curtains, wee andy's curtains are ragged and smudged, he pulls back and cums in my left ear, he gets up and leaves the living room, i stuff another kitten in my bag, i rearrange the remaining seven so that they look like a tight unit again, i put my clothes on and down my glass, the john is back, "good luck with your science fiction project, you were right: it's not about money, it's about integrity and tenacity, and also about vanity and getting laid, and putting crystal geese on your mantelpiece", he stuffs a few notes in the back pocket of my jeans, pats it, pushes me outside and slams the door, i clutch my handbag and run inside an empty telephone booth, one of the kittens is missing an ear, i crush it, i call wee andy: "hello?", "andy, crystal kittens are pretty atrocious, aren't they??", "yes they are", i hang up on that fucking ungrateful middle class cunt, i leave the telephone booth and throw the two remaining kittens in a concrete mixer.

A WONDERFUL DOG'S LIFE / i wake up and i have no idea how old i am or which season this is, but i hope it's not spring; i'm 23, i live in a junkie-infested housing scheme and the indian summer is doing its best to bring me down but it's not quite succeeding, christopher's clinging to me and i don't need anyone, and there's a big fat cat sitting on my dodgy neighbour's window sill and it's the most beautiful cat i've ever seen, i throw a beer bottle at it and it ducks just in time and then hisses at me, it's the most beautiful hiss i've ever heard; we're bored and it's wonderful cos it's like this day is gonna take years to end, but by the end of it we won't be older or more spiteful, everything will still be wonderful; the retarded flemish cook passes by our window and we call him inside and we suck his cock for free cos we're feeling generous, but he insists on giving us chocolate and dough and we don't refuse it cos that would be rude; the three of us are sitting on my bed listening to sad songs about unrequited love and the spanish civil war, i can't relate but it's gorgeous all the same; i cut my arms with a stanley knife that i brought home from the supermarket, the blood is trickling down on christopher's beautiful calves, he writes my name on his left calf with my blood, next to it he writes his own name; the retarded flemish cook starts sobbing cos he feels left out, we can't help but laugh at so much self-pity, to make up for it, we both suck his cock again; i read the retard and the illiterate rentboy one of my latest stories and they laugh at all the wrong places and christopher asks if i could refer to him as "gorgeous" rather than "illiterate" in the future, but no i can't; the gorgeous rentboy tries to sulk but he's way too cheerful to pull it off; we watch a film on the telly, it's an animation film, it's about a posh dog that runs away from his posh home to slum it, but in the end he comes to his senses and realises that warm blankets, copious meals in silver dog bowls and long walks with his good-natured owner are preferable to street violence; there's a horrible sound coming from the piss-soaked corridor: someone's whetting a knife or someone's sawing my bike in two, it's the latter, thank god; we listen to some more sad songs about awkward boys that don't fit in and bad mothers who smash furniture and china deer on their trembling children, christopher is wanking, but it's nothing to do with the content of the songs, it's to do with a picture of liam gallagher he just came across in an old music magazine; when christopher stops wanking, the retarded flemish cook starts sobbing again, when the retarded flemish cook finally stops sobbing, i resume cutting my arms with that sweet stanley knife that smells of yoghurt and rudiger's aftershave; the three of us go out to buy ice cream and feed the lively ducks in the park, this is probably the closest to innocence we'll ever get; we go to the shopping centre, i caress the goldfish that have become so big, and i greet the new wee ones; the retarded flemish cook buys me lots of red knickers and stuffed polar bears, i buy christopher a new leather bracelet and a lighter in the shape of a dolphin cos the rentboy likes tacky dolphin-shaped gadgets; i also buy a postcard of a non-performing seal and i send it to my autistic cousin who's shackled and sedated in a dreary secluded nuthouse that's infested with people who loathe his generosity and kindness, and that's the staff i'm talking about; we sit in a deserted parking lot, the indian summer sun is setting, christopher is dancing on the hood of a mercedes, the mercedes has a sticker on its rear window: "a dog's for life, not just for christmas", i'm feeling self-indulgent, i take out my black marker and black out the first "for".

NO LUCK AT THE FAIR / my dodgy neighbour's got a pillory in his garage, he's bought it from an austrian monk who used to fasten his choir boys and polish nephews to it, i am fastened to it, it's a bit humiliating, my neighbour's threatening to open the door of the garage and expose me to the scorn of the rotten twisted locals, not to mention their cocks and daggers and bitter flemish vegetables, he's angry with me cos he found out that i gave head to a dour Austrian yuppie cunt for free, it's true: last tuesday i sucked it, i did down all his bottles of german brandy and perfume first, and he bought me a seal-shaped charm and a leather jacket afterwards, he insisted on calling it wooing, i insist on calling it whoring, my dodgy neighbour calls it "fucking treachery", and that's why he's gonna let me stand here for 256 hours, he slams the door shut, opens it again, glares at me, slams it shut again, locks and bolts it one hundred times, there are quite a few days in 256 hours, i can't last that long without cock, i'm gagged, telepathy is the only means of communication left: "dear christopher, i am fastened to a pillory in my dodgy neighbour's garage. stop. how are you? stop. i feel miserable to be honest. stop. please help me escape. stop. love, delphine. stop"; outside, the flemish fish market is booming, i can hear wee andy driving a hard bargain with a kinky flemish fishmonger over four canadian groupers, it all sounds very idyllic and peaceful from where i'm standing, of course i fully well know that outside is even bleaker than my dodgy neighbour's garage, i'm just being sentimental, when the fishmongers start to pack up their stalls and wads and codlings, i send the illiterate rentboy another message: "christopher, it's me again. stop. did you not get my last message? stop. maybe you are fastened to a pillory as well?! stop. i am hungry and i need a shot of rum. stop. we've run out of toilet paper and fags. stop. buy some BEFORE you liberate me. stop. thanks. stop"; i'm humming an oasis song and watching the blood on the windscreen of my dodgy neighbour's jaguar dry, i hear someone unlock the door, it isn't christopher, it's my neighbour, he wants to arsefuck me and punch me in the face with a tacky fibre effigy of the patron saint of flemish ex-colonial scum; "why are you looking so sad?" he asks and ungags me, "because i haven't written a decent story in two days, and also: last night at the fair a vicious russian cow killer raped me behind the merry-go-round, and afterwards he threw balls in the mouths of flemish ogres and he won me a sickly goldfish, but then he wanted to rape me again, so i ran, i was carrying the wee plastic bag with the depressed goldfish in it and i ran so hard all the water spilled on my blouse, the goldfish choked and everyone could see my nipples", my dodgy neighbour arsefucks me and punches me in the face, he leaves again, but at least now i can talk to the dust on his crossbows or to the spider under his worktable, i don't feel like talking, i'll be a hunchback if i have to stand like this much longer, no one will want to pay a hunchback for a blowjob, maybe they'll rub me for good luck, my dodgy neighbour enters the garage, he unfastens me and carries me upstairs, we're watching a documentary about bent australian politicians, my neighbour's rubbing my spine and rambling about his son's heart transplant and about french marksmen who are supposedly ganging up on him, i down a shot of german cognac, put on my clothes and stagger outside, there's a minging russian hobo sitting on my doorstep, i can't tell him what i've just been through cos i don't know the russian word for "pillory", so instead i tell him about my dodgy neighbour's son's heart transplant, and i also tell him that my best friend wee andy got ripped off by a greedy flemish fishmonger this morning, and that i've lost my faith in telepathy.

GERMAN BRIEFNESS AND A BUCKET FULL OF EELS / i've got the late shift at the supermarket, which means that i can gleefully create pools of tomato sauce, cranberry juice and smashed peas, bathe in them, and use them to paint vulgar poems on the ladders and shelves; nobody will mind, at least not til tomorrow, and tomorrow's so far away; apart from a few demanding old cunts who are distressed because the wrapping of their familiar brand of chocolate has changed, the bloody supermarket's deserted, i jump on top of the pallet i'm supposed to stack: beans in tomato sauce, asparagus jars, milk bottles, ocean spray, peas and carrots, jam jars and tinned murder; i kick one side of the pallet onto the floor, it's quite spectacular, there's a pool of tomato sauce, cranberry juice, buttermilk and smashed carrots covering a fair bit of supermarket ground, such a ghastly colour though, i splash about for a bit, but i don't enjoy myself, so i take a piece of broken glass and slit my wrists, it still looks ghastly, and i'm discouraged, and i don't wanna bleed to death in a pool of tomato sauce, cranberry juice, buttermilk and smashed carrots; the sturdy security geezer, the one who oozes safety and wears a ponytail, comes over to me, he asks me if i'm ok, of course i'm not ok, i'm bleeding to death in a ghastly pool of tomato sauce, cranberry juice, buttermilk and smashed carrots; how could i be ok? the sturdy security geezer who oozes safety carries me to the infirmary, "don't bother, i'm beyond repair", rudiger cleanses my wounds whilst the sturdy security geezer who oozes safety gently strokes my hair and tells me that everything's gonna be alright and yes of course he loves the smiths, doesn't everyone?! rudiger is looking at my wrists rather intently and uneasily, there's a huge pool of blood on the floor, you could drown a lamb in it, but why would you? "you need stitches", "hmm", "i'll drive you to the hospital", "hmm", i hate having to part from the sturdy security geezer who oozes safety, but i guess if i ever want to bleed in his arms again, i'd better get stitched up, "i fear i'm dying", "no you're not, shut up", ach that lovely german briefness, how truly comforting it is; rudiger puts on the radio, aaaah, it's a chubby innocent doe-eyed indie orphan boy, how marvelous, how very ungerman; "this is not the road to the hospital", "no it isn't, shut up", that horrible german briefness, how truly unsettling it is; "fucking gestapo cunt", that never fails to wind him up, and he punches me in the face gestapo-style; we arrive at rudiger's house, it's cosy, there's a fat german cat sitting on the window sill, it's scowling at me, i hiss at it and it runs off; i'm still bleeding, "i'm still bleeding", "don't worry, i have bandages and disinfectant inside", ach that wonderful german efficiency, how truly comforting it is; rudiger pours me a glass of wine, red wine, "i thought germans only drank beer", "don't be silly", the phone's ringing, the supermarket phone, i forgot it was still in the pocket of my smudged apron, it's my boss, he's calling from home, "should i pick it up?", "yes, pick it up", "now what?", "where the fuck are you??? i just received a phone call from rosaline, she says you went home", "i'm not home, i'm at rudiger's, i'm bleeding to death, a customer attacked me", "why?? what happened??", "something to do with those new chocolate wrappings, i guess he doesn't like them... i don't like them either to be honest, the colours are too loud and the print's too small", "why are you at rudiger's? shouldn't you be at a hospital?", "i am at a hospital", "but you said you were at rudiger's", "yes, no, fuck off, i hope you choke on your roast beef tonight", and i break the connection and throw the supermarket phone in a bucket that's standing by the telly, it's filled with eels, how odd, "why is there a bucket full of eels standing by the telly?", "a hobby of mine", "putting buckets of eels by the telly???", "fishing", "nazi scum", he punches me in the face again nazi-style, and then continues bandaging my wrists.

WEE ANDY'S PUNCTUATION IS BETTER THAN MINE / i sure miss wee andy, he doesn't want to see me anymore, he reckons i'm too sleazy, i'm corrupting him, i stole his innocence and lots of bollocks like that, sod the middle class twat, i hope he dies of boredom, the bloody wee coward couldn't even say it in my face, he had to write it in a letter, it was full of spelling mistakes i should add, he sure rejected me politely, but that only makes it worse, goes to show he really doesn't give a fuck; i'm sitting on wee andy's rooftop, i've spent my best moments on rooftops, usually rooftops from people i love, i get a little nostalgic sitting here, but fuck that, there's nothing to be nostalgic about, it was all bad, they were all rotten and twisted, there was the telly and my smiths tape, but apart from that it was horrible, and i'm still waiting for it to end, and because i've had "such a hard life", his words, not mine; i refuse to take any responsibility, i just want to slash my puny body and suck dodgy cock until it kills me, and in between the slashing sprees and compulsive shagging, i write totally inappropriate shit about being raped by relatives and whatnot and they get gradually more vulgar and more incoherent, wee andy read them cos i plastered his bedroom walls with all my stories and he couldn't bloody well ignore them; it's a shame all my friends are illiterate rentboys and retarded flemish cooks; i tried to teach christopher to read but i'm not very patient and he's not very bright, that project only lasted an hour, well at least he knows the alphabet, and he can write his name, even if it's in a totally crippled handwriting, i'm glad he came to his senses and went back to the streets selling his fat arse, i'm sure them rotten twisted adults will shag the fat off him in no time, either that or some psychopath will arsefuck him with a paring gouge and shoot an arrow into his groin, which will rob him of his appetite, as paring gouges tend to do; my poor traumatised rentboy, i know he loves sucking vicar cock, and i know he's more attached to his nefarious pimp gavin than he is to me, but i miss listening to oasis b-sides with him, both of us wallowing in self-pity, both of us loathing literature and despising conceited yuppie scum, but most of all i miss his wanking over liam gallagher pics, his gaze so serious, so intense; his boner was absolutely gorgeous, it only ever raises itself like that for liam, only for liam, definitely not for some sleazy vicar; i try to avoid rapists, but there are so many, it's like trying to avoid a tree in a forest, i'll probably never get used to being gagged tied kicked slapped arsefucked etc, it's just that they can so easily kill me, it's not a comforting thought, and as much as i love living the life of a whore, i'd rather not die as one, it's neither heroic nor romantic, i want to die by my own hand, somewhere in 2008, january or february, i can't make up my mind, january or february? gun or knife? sea or tree? pills or rat poison? jumping in front of a train that's heading for france or jumping from a hotel morrissey once stayed at? so many dilemmas, possibilities more like it, i've really warmed to the idea of suicide, and now that i've written it down so explicitly there's no way i'm backing out, i don't bluff, i talk lots of shite but my shite is more truthful than yours; i stole a stuffed duck from the bloody supermarket, i badly want to shag it, i don't know why, it just looks so sexual, like everything else really, i wish i was a dog, then i could hump legs and lamp posts and people would think it funny rather than sick, lately i've been shagging lots of inanimate objects, i'm a bit bored of sex with people, it's cos none of youse sleazy cunts can keep your gob shut during the shag, language is a huge turn-off, and it's not like them pervs are particularly witty, eloquent or tender; it's either threats or clichés, and sometimes i can't tell the clichés from the threats, so stuffed ducks it is now; wee andy is sunbathing in his back garden, the wee pale scottish cunt will never get a tan, what does the vain poof want a tan for anyway? indie poofs are supposed to be pale, surely the image-conscious cunt must know this: "STOP SUNBATHING, IT'LL RUIN YOUR MUSICAL CAREER!!" the wee cunt looks up at me and sees me gyrating on his roof, he gets all dramatic like i'm about to kill myself, the wee bored middle class twat just can't resist a scene, "please, come down, delphine, we can work this out, we can still be friends", he's so full of himself, this has got absolutely nothing to do with him, i just love his rooftop: "i saw morrissey on the telly last night, it was the first time i ever heard him talk, it was amazing, andy, he was so kind, and so modest, and he speaks so softly, and his quiff looked so good, i'm so full of love for him now, what to do though with so much love?? to quote my surrogate father himself: why did you give me so much love in a loveless world when there is no one i can turn to to unlock all this love?... maybe i should jump after all", of course i'm only saying this to bait the wee gullible cunt, i don't want to ruin his smug patio with my smashed skull, that wouldn't be nice, "please come down, delphine, we can talk about it", "about your letter?? by the way, your spelling sucks", "by the way, your punctuation sucks", "cheeky cunt... go on, spell 'punctuation'", "p-u-n-c-t-u-a-t-i-o-n", "hmm, spell 'haemorrhage'", "h-a-e-m-o-r-h-a-g-e", "WRONG, there are two 'r's in 'haemorrhage'", "it's dormice, not dormouses", "i knew that, i was taking some poetic liberty, sad cunt", i'm pissed off now, "damn you, you bloody pedantic middle class poof with your supposed flawless punctuation, i have more sex than you, so i win", "i have lots of sex", "no you haven't, deluded tosser, twice a week isn't what i would call lots", "at least i'm having sex with someone whom i love and who loves me too", "no she doesn't, wee naïve cunt; at least i'm having sex with stuffed ducks who don't pretend they love me", "they can't pretend, they're dead", "maybe they're pretending to be dead!!" we spend the rest of the afternoon bickering about punctuation and stuffed ducks until the sun sets and the wee cunt has a wee date with his middle class slag, he cruelly rejects me for the umpteenth time, and the rooftop is cold and lonely now, i slide down a rainpipe and walk home, home where my morrissey is looking ever so tormented and self-conscious, spelling is more important than punctuation, and i'm sure my surrogate father would agree.

NEITHER TORMENTED NOR RELIGIOUS / i'm reading a book at a ghastly church cos it was the only quiet place i could think of and i was too tired to walk to the ghastly disused station, i secretly hope some old religious cunt is gonna save me, but the church's deserted, which is just as well cos i don't want to be saved by some old religious cunt, there's no way that he's gonna let me listen to joy division cos ian curtis killed himself and there's some law against suicide in catholic households; i hate the book and i wish i'd brought my walkman with me, i fucking hate myself, and i wish i'd brought my scalpel with me but a candelabrum will do, i'm just about to impale myself when i see a perv coming towards me, i can tell he's a perv cos he's old and fat and he only entered the church to chat up fucked-up orphan girls, when i ask him about the dour cunt on the wall he doesn't know his name so he can't be all that religious, the dour cunt on the wall is luke and he's fucking famous; and then he asks me what i'm reading but i can tell that he doesn't give a fuck so i'm not gonna bother answering, he can have the book, he can wank all over it for all i care, i'm too gloomy to concentrate on the words and i'm gonna be gloomy for the rest of my life, every time i read a paragraph it feels like being stabbed in the belly with a dull stanley knife, there's not enough commas in the book anyway; he's put a hand on my thigh, can't he see that i'm minging? can't he smell that i haven't washed myself or changed clothes for too long? it can't be healthy to touch me, my body's covered with layers of dried-up spunk, blood, mucus and whatnot, millions of animals crawling in and out of all my orifices, my hair's greasy and my eyes are festering and it looks like i'm crying the whole time, but it's just fluid running from my eyes, and the perv's drying my tears with a paper handkerchief but they're not tears, and he doesn't really want to console me, he wants a cheap shag, but i let him touch my face cos his hands are big and warm and i'm really aroused by now, even though part of me hates his guts and another part of me is scared cos the perv is staring at me with cold reptile eyes and he's stopped caressing my face and he wants to take me to his home, and i can take the dog with me if i want, i don't tell him that it's not my dog, it's just some scruffy orphan beast who's been following me around ever since i patted his head and gave him some stale bread this morning, i haven't even given him a name yet, "what's its name?", "luke", i sit in the passenger seat and luke's sitting on my lap, we drive for a long time, i catch a glimpse of wee andy, he's sitting on a bench reading one of his insipid yankee novels, he's looking beautiful and carefree, like he doesn't give a fuck about autumn, like he doesn't care that i'm about to get raped by an old fat cold-blooded perv who's not religious at all, i rap the window but he doesn't hear it and the cunt's driving too fast anyway; there are seagulls circling his house, not a good sign at all, the dog has to stay outside he tells me, the house is big, there are lots of paintings on the wall and when he sees me looking at them he tells me that he himself painted them, he's a big fucking artist and he just got back from new york and he expects me to give him some kind of compliment but they're fuckawful paintings and new york doesn't really exist anyway, i ask him who's the dour cunt in that picture and it's his father and he was an actor, he once played van gogh in a french film about gauguin, but he doesn't seem very tormented to me, why didn't they give him the gauguin part? we drink a few glasses of red wine, it's making me really drowsy, maybe i shouldn't have done those pills i stole from wee andy's, the wee cunt's epileptic and i've been drinking so much lately that i've become an epileptic myself, it's scary, every time i look at the sky my tongue tries to choke me; the perv has ripped off my clothes and he's looking really angrily at me, like i'm the one who just ripped off his clothes, he fucks me hard and loveless and somewhere in the house there's a bird singing, and it's jarring and unsettling, like being confronted with someone you used to hang out with before you turned evil; i'm too drunk to come and i'm too drowsy to fake it, so basically i'm just lying there watching myself getting fucked by some big artist who's neither religious nor tormented, so i don't really like him all that much, and also he's punching me in the face and it hurts but i'm too drowsy to panic let alone run away; he gets bored of my genitals after an hour and he pretends i'm no longer here, he just stands there in the middle of the living room admiring his own fuckawful paintings; i get dressed, i walk into the corridor and take his wallet out of his leather jacket; luke wags his scruffy tail when he sees me but he stops wagging it when i kick his scruffy emaciated body, i kick it real hard, and then i start to cry, but it's just fluid running from my eyes, i hitchhike and i get a lift from a snotty middle class geezer, luke is sleeping on my lap, i ask the geezer if he knows the artist who just quite brutally shagged me, and of course he does but he doesn't believe that the guy shagged me, cos he's "fucking famous" and i am scum, and why would a guy with so much money chat up minging orphan girls at churches? it doesn't make sense he says, and then i stop listening and fall asleep, i stagger out of the car and luke follows me cos he hasn't really got a choice, we walk back to the church to fetch the book but it's gone, so instead i take a few catholic pamphlets but they're poorly written and quite harsh, i stuff them into wee andy's post box and i hope they fucking haunt him.

SAVING WEE ANDY WHO THINKS HE'S SAVING DELPHINE WHO THINKS SHE'S SAVING CHRISTOPHER / "oh christopher, what have they done to you?!!" my tender rentboy's stumbled into the bedsit bleeding from every pore, burst mouth, broken nose, all of him bruised and battered, he's twisting and sobbing on my floor and i'm kneeling beside him, i'm stroking his hair and its all sticky with blood and spunk, there's a gaping wound in the middle of his skull and it's gushing, i can't think of anything comforting to say except that it's gonna be alright, but that's a lie, "who did this to you?" but he doesn't answer, he doesn't talk, he takes my hand and chews on it, which i find a little odd, but now's not the time to start dissing all his peculiar habits; if it wasn't for wee andy, christopher and i would be enjoying swaying and selling our most important assets, but no, the wee moralist cunt had to poison us with his values, making us feel like freaks, like we are the rotten and twisted ones, he almost got us believe that what we do is wrong, he proper fucked with our minds, the wee righteous cunt, and ever since we can't help but slash and punch and stab ourselves after every shag, but christopher's wounds aren't self-inflicted, he's terrified and he's not faking it, tears are rolling over his swollen face, they mingle with the blood and snot and then drop from his chin onto his oasis t-shirt, he's got a boner, i feel like a perv for noticing it, but then it's really hard not to, i bet the rotten twisted adults who did this to him will be justifying themselves by saying he got a boner, which means he enjoyed it; much like her cunt was wet and throbbing, which means she wanted it, but my cunt is always wet and throbbing, it doesn't mean i want fists or bottles or knives shoved into it, it means that i'm not dead, and i'm thinking necrophilia, and i hope someone will shag me when i'm dead, and i'm picturing the scene: young skinny girl with slit wrists found naked on her bed, i hope they all have a go, i want to be useful to the end and after, bollocks, i just wanna be buried with fresh spunk splashed on my cold pale body; christopher is still sobbing, i've taken him in my arms, i have to save him, i promised i would, and if i lose christopher to the rotten twisted adults i might as well join them myself, i'm having terrible thoughts, i'm thinking about killing christopher just because it would be so much easier than bringing him back, i wish he'd talk, i wish he'd stop sobbing, i call wee andy, goes to show how desperate i am, "andy, it's christopher, he's been beaten up, it's serious, we need your help", "i'm not coming over to you, last time i came round you shoved a garden rake up my arse", "oh bloody hell, it was only the stick, get over it, wee oversensitive cunt, this is not about you, it's about christopher, the boy you supposedly fancy, he's fucking dying, mate, get your wee arse over here", and i hang up, and we wait for the wee useless cunt, i'm lulling christopher and humming manics songs about prostitution and abuse of all kinds, i find those songs much more comforting than jaunty pop songs about little middle class people with little middle class solutions to little middle class problems, and so does christopher, the wee shallow poof finally arrives and he just stands there staring down on us with his big innocent eyes, they are twitching, his teeth are clattering and his whole body's trembling, "pull yourself together, mate, this is what we deal with every day, now either you can go back to your safe cozy comfortable middle class life, or you can help me patch up christopher and find the bastards who did this to him, what's it gonna be?", "i... i... i... ", "i spy with my little eye a wee scared middle class cunt who'd rather gyrate like a spazwit in front of his full length mirror in his huge luxurious bedroom in his fucking peaceful bourgeois neighbourhood where there are no signs of any violent excesses or whimpering junkies than help out his two only friends", "but i don't know how to help", "well, just staying here and helping me put christopher in the bed would be a start, wee inadequate cunt", "could you stop throwing abuse at me, it's kinda hurtful",

"HURTFUL??? HURTFUL??? i'll show you hurtful if you don't shut your gob, wee oversensitive cunt", i do feel bad about treating wee andy this badly, but if i didn't, the wee apathetic cunt would just gyrate his life away, so basically i'm saving him, and christopher, though i'm sure the wee arrogant cunt thinks its the other way around.

NO FLEMISH MERCY / my dodgy neighbour is telling me all the ways to kill a person with your bare hands, cos before he was retired he was a wine merchant, but before he was a wine merchant he was in the army, there's no one i want to go to prison for, and i'm definitely not going to prison for brutally slaughtering a lazy talentless spineless conceited corporate cock who sits in a meadow every sunday with other lazy talentless spineless conceited corporate cocks smoking spliff and reading each other cheesy middle class poetry, he's sitting in that meadow right now, he's not picking up his mobile cos he doesn't want the fucked-up orphan girl to corrupt him and his middle class slags, besides didn't i promise him i was gonna stop stalking him and take care of a wee fucking animal or save the third world instead?! but stalking the sheffielder cunt is much more entertaining than taking care of some fucking ungrateful mammal that's gonna take an instant dislike to me and bite me, so that's me again forced into being the obsessive manipulative fucked-up stalker bitch tart slag sex monster, leave me the fuck alone, but all i want is for him to talk to me (and shag me and adopt me), that's not bloody unreasonable or demanding or anything; so after having called him 200 times and having listened 200 times to "hi, i'm afraid i'm not around but please leave your name and number and i'll get back to you as soon as possible", and after having read 200 spiteful messages into his bloody mobile i was so pissed off that there was nothing left to do than go out and get fucked by the most repulsive cock i know, and the most repulsive cock i know happens to live next door; and the most repulsive cock i know is bragging about all the niggers he shot in the congo and all the black bitches he knocked up- all of them underage- and all the rookies he pissed on and all the poofs he beat up and all the police pigs he bribed etc etc, we're drinking geneva- which he insists on calling "flemish gin", but it's stronger and filthier than gin- in wee glasses that have ghastly flemish churches on them, and i ask my neighbour has he been inside that church, but it's not a church, it's an abbey, and no he hasn't; i'm straddling the seventy-three year old cunt who can't even remember my name cos i'm sick of his war stories and sick of him telling me how sorry he feels for me and that he wants to help me and that having sex with a seventy-three year old pig will surely heal my soul and body, if i could just relax and let his hands "rub off all the sorrow and filth"; but it isn't working, i feel filthier than before, and i didn't feel sad but i do now, the cum redeems him, i come in flemish, i always come in flemish when i'm out of my head on geneva, i'd rather not hear him come, it sounds too much of death throes; he's still fingering me and i'm about to come again when that headless cuckoo beast pops out and announces fuckall really, it pops out every quarter, it's a proper turnoff, as are his old man's slippers and the flemish abbeys on the shot glasses; i wanna go home, anywhere is more home than here, no matter how cosy his wee house is supposed to be it's still a fucking perv's lair and i'm not staying, unless you pour me another glass of flemish gin and give me another flemish cum, which he does, i down the glass, he pushes me onto the couch and eats my cunt until i scream out "genade", which is flemish for 'mercy'; i feel quite shattered now- for want of a better word- and i don't think i can ever go back to fucking normal men now, which is just as well cos normal men fuck like women; christopher is sleeping on my bed, he's sucking on a stuffed rabbit's ear, i go sit in my shower tray and call that unfaithful sheffielder cunt but i'm too pissed to form the number, so i call the suicide hotline number instead and i tell the geezer on the other end of the line that i'm seriously considering taking an overdose of tranquilisers and slitting my wrists and he wants to know what colour my nipples are.

FUCK YOU TO DEATH / there's a spiteful cunt on the bus staring at my tits and bawling me out, but it's like he's bawling out my tits, so i really don't give a fuck, and the spiteful cunt's my father, and i really don't give a fuck about my father; i get off at the library and the spiteful cunt follows me though i'm sure it's not where he was headed for; the library is full of sad old drunkards and none of them is reading a book, but i'm not a moralist bastard, and most of these books are unreadable anyway, and most of these writers are cynical middle class twats anyway, and most of these sad old drunkards are illiterate anyway; i sit myself at a small table from where i can see the time, cos time is money and i'm shagging the retarded flemish cook at three pm for a whole lot of money, the spiteful cunt is still yelling at my tits, though he tries to keep his voice down, which goes to show that much of his rage is acted and therefore not scary at all, but still annoying, and do you mind, i'm trying to write a story, and you might as well make yourself useful and come up with a title cos i'm too tired to be a smart cunt, and i don't see the point anymore, at least that's how i'm feeling right now, but i might be feeling completely different in five minutes, and i can't wait for these five minutes to pass, and then they're gone and the gloom is fleeting, and the spiteful cunt has come up with a title: "fuck you to death", at least that's what i think he says cos he's slurring the words like the sad old alcoholic he is, "fuck you to death" is as good a title as any, so i continue writing my fuck you to death story, but there's a skinny geezer coming over to the table, and it's wee andy, and i'm not really embarrassed about my father, but i still run over to meet him before he can reach the table, wee andy smells of oatmeal and roses, he looks like he's just had rough sex with a retired biology teacher, but of course he hasn't, and i ask him if he thinks "fuck you to death" is a good title for a story, but he thinks it sucks, blame the sad old drunkard over there, he's the one who came up with it; i'm relieved when the wee middle class cunt is gone, though i miss the smell of oatmeal and roses, all my father oozes is calvados and lame titles, and him calling me a useless slag is not doing much for my self-esteem, but then the cunt nods off and that's me out of there and into a seedy pub with a deceptive name waiting for the flemish retard and i can't think of many things i want to do with his money, and that's a depressing thought, but then i think of all the disappointing indie albums i can buy with it, and that really cheers me up, but no not really, and maybe i'll shag him for free then; it seems like i'm being stood up by a retarded flemish cook, which is a whole new experience for me, just as well, i'm too drunk to lift my hand and caress retarded flesh anyway; the pub is full of sad old drunkards and dour catholic monsters, and most of the dour catholic monsters are junkies, at least that's what christopher told me, but he's an illiterate rentboy so he was probably making it up cos he's full of spite and he blames catholics- all of them- for his whoring ways; my dodgy neighbour enters the pub and it's odd to see him here, so far away from our neighbouring houses, it doesn't make him any more attractive, he's chatting up some fat old german ex-whore; outside it's pouring, there's a spiteful cunt sitting on a bench, he doesn't seem to give a fuck about the rain, he's strumming his guitar and singing spiteful songs about a stuck-up slag who stalks him cos she thinks he's her father, but he's not etc etc, and i hope the bastard drowns.

SUPERMARKET MAYHEM / yes, yes, yes, it was me who painted manics lyrics on all the rock'n'roll star vacuum cleaners, it was me who told the customers they could shop for free every friday between two and four pm, it was me who trashed all those greatest hits albums and replaced them with marion and the locust, it was me who freed all the seals and tigers and camels at the zoo and let them loose in your office, it was me who smeared my blood on the showcased television sets, it was me who put dead rodents in the milk bottles, it was me who dragged all those dead animals out of that sickly refrigerator and i buried them nice and proper i even might have prayed in one of my weak theatrical moods, it was me who hid on the bottom shelf slashing yuppie heels with my favourite scalpel, it was me who dropped all those soup cans and tinned meat and boxes and bottles and dime store novels on top of the french delegation and as they were bleeding to death i sprayed them with whipped cream until them bloody yuppies all blended into this pink mass of broken glass, vegetables, piss, blood, soup, insipid chapters and dead animals, it was me who did all those things and more, now please give me the sack, but of course them bloody cunts found out that it was not me at all, it was peter peter jolly wife beater, and they thought it exceptionally noble of me that i had been willing to take the blame, and i got a medal and a fucking promotion; i don't want a fucking medal, and you can shove that promotion up yer arse, i accepted the medal cos it's the only medal i'm likely to ever receive, it was embarrassing, they even took a picture of the talentless minger and i got the rest of the day off and i wasted the rest of the day getting pissed on cheap red wine, listening to oasis b-sides, wanking over my morrissey pic, talking to a cocky sparrow, liberating seals and tigers and camels, sucking ex-wine merchant cock, comforting the retarded flemish cook but only cos i want his money and i'll gladly dry a few tears, flash a pair of tits and suck some dodgy cock for a few disappointing indie cds, and then my sheffielder angel walked up to me and he covered my puny body with my black sweater and i shouted abuse at him cos i'd rather be raped than comforted, and i know it's fucked up and i don't care, youse cunts can take away my notebooks and fountain pen, i'll use my blood to write, i'll cover the whole city with obscenities, i've done it before and i'll do it again, blood-soaked obscenities about bloodthirsty relatives, and only a very vicious blow to the skull could stop me, don't take that as a challenge you fucking perv; i bump into the venomous busker and i suggest we write a warped duet about incest together, "it's been done before" he says, do you always have to discourage me you spiteful miserable dwarf? but the cunt just laughs, and then i go over to noel's but the dour mancunian servant won't let me in, so i sneak in through the hedge at the back and a depressed goldfish with the big accusatory eyes is leisurely swimming in a giant fishbowl and i'm well jealous, i'll tell you that much, i'm about to impale the smug cunt when i spot wee andy coming out of a pub: "andy, wait, andy, please listen, can we go back from obsessive stalker-victim to being friends, i want to listen to the smiths with you and moan about my sheffielder angel, no more crushing beer bottles between my thighs, no more crotch grabbing, no more frightening letters, no more broken windows", "and no more rodents?", "and no more rodents, andy, i promise", we stare at each other for a while and start to giggle, and we never stop giggling, and we listen to the smiths the whole day, and wee andy gyrates like morrissey, and we throw imaginary gladioli out his bedroom window and it is a bright day, and we forget all about abusive grandfathers and restraining orders and sucking dodgy cock, and all is bliss.

200 POEMS,300 LETTERS AND 24 SPLINTERS IN A JAR / there are glass splinters in my chest, i'm going over to wee andy, he'll pull them out, how did they get there? hmm, it's a bit embarrassing, last night i had to jerk off a really repulsive glaswegian hairdresser, he picked me up at eight pm and drove me to a sleazy coastal motel, we didn't talk in the car, i leafed through his bible and occasionally rubbed his crotch, he looked very determined and very cross, he parked the car at the disused prison and from there we walked to the motel, the motel was called "stella maris", but it read "ella maris" cos the two first letters weren't lit, the room was small and murky, it smelled of my dodgy neighbour's sweaty testicles and of terrified pheasants, there were posters of lecherous topless ballet dancers on the walls, and there was also a poster of a naked french vixen sucking a banana and squinting at the camera, it wasn't very alluring, anyway, that glaswegian cunt scoffed at my haircut, ripped off my clothes and shoved his fist up my arse, then later he painted atrocious butterflies on my chest and belly, "who the fuck do you think you are? charlie manson?" i shouted at him, he slapped my minge and shoved his other fist up my arse, i burst into tears, he pushed me off the bed and kicked me in the back, i crawled into the black bathtub and scrubbed away those hideous insects, he entered the ghastly bathroom and pissed on me, i didn't mind cos piss is like turpentine, the butterflies evaporated, i was stark white again, he punched me in the face, i was smeared with blood again, i staggered back into the room and looked out the window, there were three hedgehogs crossing the motorway, i thought that hedgehogs were solitary, mind, i'm quite myopic, so they might have been hares or toddlers, the glaswegian hairdresser took out his scissors and stabbed me in the groin, i tried to run but i tripped over a beach ball, i fell on my collar bone, i whimpered for a while and then i got up, the glaswegian hairdresser was smoking a fag like nothing had happened, when i made for the door he ran towards it and blocked it, i was terrified, i was so terrified i grabbed an empty beer bottle, i smashed it against the wall and cut my chest to appall him, it worked, he backed away, i opened the door and ran out of the motel, i ran for hours, i entered my bedsit, hugged the illiterate rentboy, downed a bottle of spanish rum, clutched a brick, clutched my left tit, clutched the illiterate rentboy's fringe, downed a bottle of german cognac and collapsed in my shower tray; i knock on wee andy's door, he's not home, i sit myself on his doorstep and write two hundred slanderous poems about my mother's voracious minge and three hundred spiteful letters to my sheffielder angel, the churlish coastal sun is setting, i take out my mobile and call that wee unfaithful twat: "delphine!", "chest, glass, splinters, hairdresser, very, malicious, scared, i, am", i pretend to be traumatised, "where are you??", it always works, "doorstep, your, bleeding, terrified, help, splinters, glass", "hold on, delph, i'm on my way", i smoke a fag and count the stubs that are lying on the pavement, and then wee andy arrives, i hug him tightly, he strokes my hair and kisses my chin, we go inside, i take off my blouse, wee andy fetches disinfectant and wads and a needle, he tries hard not to stare at my tits, "you can fondle my tits if you want", "i don't want to fondle your tits, i want to remove these splinters", "FINE", i sulk, wee andy shyly plucks at the glass splinters, he puts them on a green napkin, twenty-four splinters, i put them in an empty mustard jar and angrily shake the jar, they make a sad sound, we share a bottle of bourbon and ramble about graham greene and nocturnal rodents, wee andy nods off, i shake the jar until the churlish coastal sun comes up again.

APOLOGIES TO INSECT LIFE / i'm standing on my ladder stacking baby pears in light syrup, they look like the fetuses of rabbits, i show them to the corporate cunt who's standing and scowling at the bottom step of my ladder, i accidentally drop twelve jars of baby pears in light syrup on his head, he's not dead, he's saying that i did it on purpose and that i'm sacked, i burst out in tears, peter peter jolly wife beater is comforting me in his sad crippled way, pat pat, hush hush, the corporate cunt's got a huge lump on his forehead, it's much bigger than a baby pear, i ask him if i can rub it for good luck, since i'm unemployed i might need it, but the callous cunt bawls me out and points his index finger toward the exit of the supermarket; so this is how it feels to be unemployed, everything looks new and exciting, like i've just woken up from a three year coma, like i've just been arsefucked by a hirsute flemish peasant for the very first time, but it's fleeting, i slash my arms with the stanley knife since i don't need it any longer to cut open cartons and obstinate plastic wraps, after two hours of pathetic sobbing by the wee merry-go-round in the park i stop feeling sorry for myself and squander my money on flemish comics and liquorice, i'm sitting on some rich cunt's lawn, gnawing at the liquorice and trying to make sense of all these vile flemish speech bubbles, there's a ladybird sunbathing on my knee, everything's quite innocent and idyllic until the rich cunt who owns the house comes over to me and starts asking lots of inappropriate questions that i answer with inappropriate questions, eventually he invites me inside, inside is murky and cold, he asks me why i'm wearing a smudged apron? it's not an inappropriate question, so i tell him that i got sacked this morning cos i tried to bludgeon my boss to death with baby pears, he says that i can work in his pet shop if i want, but i decline cos domestic mammals depress me and being unemployed is not so bad, besides i make an awful lot of money by ripping off loaded pervs, "i see" the loaded perv says and he pours me a glass of vodka, we toast the belgian economy and down our glasses, he refills our glasses, we toast unemployment and i down my glass, since he doesn't refill it i resume gnawing at the liquorice, the perv asks for a piece of my liquorice, but he makes it sound like a dirty word so i say no; we watch a french flick, actually it's american but it's dubbed, paul newman sounds like a french porn actor; after the flick we fuck on his immaculate lawn, when he lays me down i can feel ladybirds squash against my spine, other more fortunate ones crawl into my ears and nostrils, so this is how it feels to be buried alive; the loaded perv licks my cunt until the sun's so big and relentless that all the white houses seem to quiver and fade before my eyes, when i come ten more ladybirds die, they don't scream, they don't even pop, the perv asks me to stop rambling about insects and to suck his cock on the kitchen floor, and suck it one more time on the lawn when the sun starts to set; i'm giving him head on the kitchen floor, his tiles are old and cracked, i can see avenging beasts in them if i want, i can even see fetuses of avenging beasts in them if i want, his spunk tastes of raw potatoes and cold coffee; we watch another french flick that's really a dubbed american flick, but paul newman isn't in it, so i'm not all that interested, i read my flemish comics and gnaw at my liquorice, i watch the perv for a while, but it's a sad show cos he's balding and he's rubbing his bulging crotch every time one of the american bitches gets smacked up, which is all the time; after the flick we fuck one more time on his blood-stained lawn, it's not blood-stained from all the insects we crushed if that's what you think, it's blood-stained cos he cut my thighs with a carving knife; so this is how it feels to bleed to death, of course i'm not really bleeding to death, i'm just adding to the drama.

YOU CAN WATCH AND FROWN,BUT PLEASE DON'T SHRUG / oh i'm in quite deep, so deep now that it'd be foolish to even try to climb out; besides i remember the "normal" world and it was shite; this is madness, this is dangerous, this i can't control no longer, but it's better than sunday trips to dorset at any rate; i'm afraid i'm stuck with the retarded flemish cook forever, oh i know i shouldn't have accepted all those generous gifts... a car?! but i can't even drive... cds, a thousand maybe more; a horse? but i hate horses, they're awkward, big and brutal... designer clothes, jewelry, furniture, and money, so much money, cash notes coins cheques every week every day today, oh did i actually think hugging him would do to keep him generous and satisfied? naïve cunt!! but it was enough in the beginning, oh even a hand on my thigh was so precious and so expensive back then, but it soon devaluated, and i'm now having to suck his crooked cock for some bread and cheese, oh i suppose it's fair, fate, poetic justice and whatnot; and when we walk through this small malicious town hand in hand, people don't see a whore ripping off a retarded john, they see lovers.

DELPHINE IS HARASSING ME / wee andy is sleeping on his bedroom floor between his music mags, smiths cds and imaginary gladioli, i've covered his skinny body with the black sweater from sheffield sex city, the daft cunt really can't handle his drink, he passed out after two bottles of white wine, i'm still at it, yeah i'm well tough, look at him so innocent so carefree, i bet he's dreaming about headlining glasto, the vain cunt, or maybe he's dreaming about me, i've made quite an impression on him lately, what with all the stalking, that awful restraining order, breaking into his house gagging and tying him forcing him to watch me crush beer bottles between my thighs, wank with scissors, burn the soles of my feet, carve morrissey quotes on my arm, set my hair on fire, crunch wine glasses, rip my nails out, shove torches up my arse, punch myself in the face until i hear my nose crack, all my orifices bleeding festering throbbing; i know i'd be impressed if i had to watch such a spectacle, the junkie scum in my building might be self-destructive, but they're not very inventive, they bang their head against walls and cut their arms with broken glass, poor imagination i say, you want to cut down on the drugs, there are better ways to hurt yourself, more efficient ways, can't they see that? there are objects everywhere and every bloody object however dull or flat can irreversibly damage you or even kill you, of course the self-harm is often compulsive and impulsive and any knife will do, but afterwards you ponder your gaping wounds and you go out and buy new cutlery, self harm is very much like art really, it should be compulsive and impulsive and cut real deep and leave huge scars, but you can't always cut the same vein, you shouldn't always carve the same pattern, don't be so fucking self-indulgent, go out, buy new knives and scissors and razor blades, look out for new objects bricks branches bottles broken bicycles whatever, and cut away passionately fearlessly compulsively impulsively and cheerfully, and if them bourgeois middle class cunts refuse to read or watch, just tie them and gag them, shove yer slashed cunt into their faces, shove all your supposedly vulgar stories under their noses, they'll fucking well watch and read me cut slash stab punch carve wank shit come choke cry; i do feel sorry about having subjected wee andy to watch this bloody crusade against my orifices, wee andy didn't even know there are people out here that have been raped rejected and beaten so many times, that they'd rather take control and do it themselves, we'd rather hurt ourselves than take revenge or corrupt someone innocent, we are fucking noble, although i do feel like i've corrupted wee andy, i've shown him despair, twenty-three years of murky basements, fear, humiliation, anger and twisted loyalty and how i handle it, i've dragged him out of his safe smug world and confronted him with terrible tales about psycho grandfathers, abusive cousins, dodgy neighbours, kinky nightnurses and whatnot, and for once i didn't make anything up, i don't know why i told him, i guess i was just being my obnoxious exhibitionist self, or maybe i just wanted him to adopt me, tuck me in, stroke my hair, kiss my bruises, but it's turned against me, every time i visit wee andy i detect the growing cynicism in his voice, and i read his lyrics and they're all angry and ugly and twisted and wry, and he doesn't gyrate so carelessly now, and the imaginary gladioli are wilting...

CHEAP FLOUR / i can't look at the retarded flemish cook, i hate that pocket-sized head and those beady greedy eyes drowning in self-pity, no chin, no jaw, just this dribbling blubbering retarded mass, i can't believe i shagged this ugly mass that smells of cheap flour and spunk, i hate him almost as much as i hate myself, no fuck that, i hate him so much more, he's a fucking john, i don't need his money any more, i'll find someone else to rip off, someone who doesn't expect me to suck his cock in exchange, there is no such person, so we shag, i just lie on the bed pretending to be dead, but sadly i'm not, and i can hear him panting and groaning, and i can feel his spittle and spunk trickling over my face down my tits and i can feel his fingers stirring my cunt, those fingers i so badly want to cut off with my scalpel and feed to the goldfish at the shopping centre, but i don't think goldfish eat fingers, the smell of cheap flour and brownish ointments and spunk and sweat and sour milk and stale bread is doing my head in, i know it'll just stay stuck in my nose for days, no matter what i shove into it or how much i drink or how many times i break it or how many johns break it for me, he's grabbing my hair and pushing my head down to his repulsive crotch, there's no way i'm sucking smelly crooked cock today, i try to pull up my head but he forces it into that hideous mass of pubes and saggy balls, a dripping foaming stinking cock, i take it into my mouth, it's not even entirely in my mouth, just the ugly tip, but it's enough to make me retch, i can't suck on this, it's not even properly hard, so instead of sucking it i bite, it's bleeding, the retard is sobbing, fucking useless retard, if i bite your cock you hit me, even your instincts are fucked up, rotten twisted cunt, you're supposed to beat me unconscious and leave and never come back; but he doesn't, he just sits there on my bed naked, his limp sorry cock is bleeding quite heavily now and the blood is trickling on the floor, on my fucking bedsit floor, and i'm overpowered by anger again, i grab his brittle hair and i smack his head against the radiator, i punch him in the face, he doesn't even fend off the blows, he just looks persecuted, his eyes are screaming injustice, like he is the fucking victim here, but he isn't and i could punch him to death, trample him, but i don't want his ugly remains the blood fibres hair guts skin etc stuck to the floor and between the bars of my radiator, so i drag him into the piss-soaked corridor and when i see the broken glass, i can't help but slash his thin pale chest and when my anger is somewhat appeased, i push him out the window, it's only the first floor, he'll live, i watch him fall on the pavement, and the clothes and shoes and all those slutty red knickers he bought for me and all the skimpy tops and the miniskirts and the vile perfume and the disappointing indie albums i bought with his money and the fluffy bears he shoved into my cunt, i don't want them any more and this fucking spunk-infested mattress and everything his filthy fingers ever touched are poisoned and infected, my stuffed seagull, the embroidered cushions, my ian rankin novels, the oasis biography, all my towels and clothes, all those useless songs that never comforted me and only remind me of him and his smelly crooked cock and the emotional blackmail and all his bank notes and all the cripple threats and all the wry tenderness and his hideous saggy flesh, it's all going out the window, crushing the fucking retarded perv; when i go back inside my bedsit, it's as good as empty, nothing left but my smiths albums and my stereo, the room smells of cheap flour and spunk like i bloody well knew it would, when morrissey starts singing, i feel slightly less distressed, and when i slash my tits with the broken glass from the corridor, i can manage a weak smile, after a few hours i'm bathing in a pool of hair, spunk and blood; there's not an inch on my body that hasn't been brushed with the glass, some wounds are deeper than others, i'm not angry anymore, maybe i've overreacted, i'm glad i got rid of the retard though i kinda regret having thrown my bed and oasis singles out the window, i go downstairs, the retarded flemish cook is sobbing between broken furniture and disappointing indie albums and feathers and slutty knickers and whatnot, "could you please get dressed?!" but he just shakes his head wearily, like i asked him something outrageous, and i feel the anger overpowering me again, and i'm bloody well not gonna fight it, i'm gonna give in to it, if i fight it, i'll never be free, and i have to be free to liberate all those animals and to burn down all those supermarkets and to obliterate all those pervs and to slander all my relatives and to expose all politicians and to write new sleazy violent truthful stories in the margins of bland insipid false mediocre yankee novels; so i throttle the sad retard and he doesn't even struggle, i hear his windpipe crack and his eyes roll back, i throw his sorry body on the street and i pick up "definitely maybe" from between my useless broken possessions, i go back into my bedsit, i envy liam's gusto, i slash my body some more, and i know i can be just as happy and wild as my mancunian brother, just not today.

THE FUCKING UNFAITHFUL MIDDLE CLASS CUNT / sometimes i hate wee andy so much that it makes me cry, i want to hurt him badly, he's a fucking unfaithful cunt, he's not supposed to go out with other people, he's supposed to sit in his smug middle class armchair and wait for me to come round and bait him, the wee popular cunt is not home and he's not picking up his mobile phone so i break his window with a brick and i climb inside, i hate all his smug middle class plants and i eat them alive and i hope they're poisonous, and i hate his smug middle class film posters and i tear them down and i spraypaint manics quotes on his walls, he's bloody well reading another insipid moralist yankee novel and it goes out the window, and there's a pretentious art book about a pretentious art movement lying on his pretentious coffee table and they fly out the window as well, i burn his fugazi cds cos fugazi are a bunch of elitist snobs and he never listens to them anyway, i down wee andy's sorry booze supply, but i'm not nearly drunk enough, so i go into his bathroom and i down his hugo boss cologne, i take his tweezers and i start carving little stars into my cheeks, i'm silly like that, i am drunk now, i am seeing things double: two trashed armchairs, two blood-stained refrigerators, two broken television sets, two smashed cupboards etc etc; i've made a huge cozy bonfire of all his poof clothes in his backyard; i ripped his morrissey pictures off his bedroom wall cos the wee fickle churlish middle class cunt is not worthy of my surrogate father; when my anger has subsided a little, i am quite shocked to find myself amidst such a ravage, and to think that i've caused it, oh dear, but i'm not running away now, i'll wait here for the popular cunt to come back from one of his posh middle class parties which he never invites me to cos he's afraid i'm gonna do "inappropriate stuff", what a wee sad cunt, what a wee sad uneventful middle class life; i miss wee andy, i hope he gets back soon, why does he have to go out with unimaginative middle class slags, why does he have to go out at all? am i not good enough for the wee bourgeois cunt, is that it??? i'm nothing but an embarrassment to him, a living endorsement, an obsessive stalker, a bloody nutter; but surely i'm ten times more exciting than those dour prim over-privileged middle class bitches, they don't love him like i love him, they don't indulge his gyrating and yodeling, and his bloody awful indie songs, and his poof talk, and his atrocious taste in furniture, and his sentimental outbursts, and his petulance which only i find endearing; and they never tried to help him escape from the nuthouse, did they now? they didn't even know that he was at the nuthouse cos the wee miserable poof was too embarrassed to tell them, goes to show how little he trusts these bourgeois bastards; then why does he have to go out with them??? they'll never take him to the zoo and drop him in the artificial arctic polar bear pond, and they won't buy him plastic dolphins, and they won't give him an asian otter for his birthday, and they won't busk with him cos middle class cunts don't busk, and they're not interested in all his obscure indie concept albums about cold war, and i bet they don't write about him, not this passionately, not this desperately, and they don't trash his house; and they'll never burn it down, cos these deluded middle class cunts reckon property's sacred; they fill wee andy's head with ugly middle class ambitions, they're bloody well poisoning him, thank god he's got me to show him what life's really about, but do you think the wee cunt's any grateful? far from it, restraining orders and petty threats are all i get, but i won't give up on wee andy, he's my best friend and he's got beautiful straight indie hair and he reads my stories and he strokes my hair when i'm sad, i punch him a lot but he always forgives me; i can hear the front door open, wee andy enters the living room and he looks at me slightly bemused, only slightly, the wee cunt is pissed, he's staggering towards me, he's stupidly grinning, he looks around at the middle class debris and he says: "delphine, you're smashing", and then he passes out on the floor between the mashed furniture, broken glass, crushed porcelain deer, ashes of insipid moralist yankee novels, tattered poof scarves, wood splinters, and blood-stained indie cds; i put a blanket over the wee drunkard, i kiss his brow and i go back to my dreary bedsit.